"I was instantly fascinated by *Bright and Dangerous Objects*, which uses the backdrops of undersea welding and a hypothetical expedition to Mars to deftly explore ideas of independence, grief, motherhood, and romantic relationships and how they shape one woman's life. . . . This is an original, inventive, and incredibly enjoyable book. I loved it."

—**LYDIA KIESLING**, author of *The Golden State*

"*Bright and Dangerous Objects* is written in a beautiful voice—it's warm, self-deprecating, lonely. The characters face impossible decisions, and they face them the way we all do, wildly, blindly. It's a book I'll remember."

—**SARA MAJKA**, author of *Cities I've Never Lived In*

"Mackintosh has written a beauty. If you've ever weighed two different eternities in your hand and had to choose which to love most, this book is yours."

—**DEB OLIN UNFERTH**, author of *Barn 8*

Published by Tin House, Portland, Oregon

Distributed by W. W. Norton & Company

Library of Congress Cataloging-in-Publication Data

Names: Mackintosh, Anneliese, author.
Title: Bright and dangerous objects / Anneliese Mackintosh.
Description: Portland, Oregon : Tin House, [2020]
Identifiers: LCCN 2020013156 | ISBN 9781951142100 (paperback) | ISBN 9781951142117 (ebook)
Classification: LCC PR6113.A2648 B75 2020 | DDC 823/.92--dc23
LC record available at https://lccn.loc.gov/2020013156

First US Edition 2020
Printed in the USA
Interior design by Diane Chonette

www.tinhouse.com

BRIGHT

AND

DANGEROUS

OBJECTS

ANNELIESE MACKINTOSH

 TIN HOUSE / Portland, Oregon

For Apollo and Socrates

To light a candle is to cast a shadow. . .

—URSULA K. LE GUIN, *A Wizard of Earthsea*

PART ONE

1

"It's incredible," I tell James. "I'm sitting here with you, but I'm looking light-years away."

We're at St. Agnes Head, one of the best Dark Sky sites in Cornwall. "Some of these stars no longer exist," I say. "They're already dead."

James takes a swig of whisky.

The moon is in its first-quarter phase. If I keep the binoculars steady, I can make out grey patches on its surface. They're lava plains, but early astronomers mistook them for oceans, so they've got wonderful names: Sea of Serenity, Sea of Crises, Sea That Has Become Known.

"This place is so quiet," James says. "Hard to believe how much has happened on the ground under our feet. You know, St. Agnes Head was once an artillery range?"

"Wow," I say. "I've found Mars." Somehow, in spite of my interest in space, I've always managed to miss Mars. But here it is, completely unmistakable, a tarnished two-pence piece in the sky.

James walks away from me.

"Don't you want to see it?"

"In a minute. You know, this heathland is an ideal habitat for spiders."

It's almost pitch black, so I'm not sure how James is expecting to see spiders, but he gets like this after a few drinks. Finds himself a preposterous mission to embark on. I suppose we're alike in that respect.

I point the binoculars southwards again, but Mars has disappeared. It doesn't help that I'm shivering, and when the lenses shake, the sky looks like television static. I take a bottle of peppermint vodka out of my pocket. I first tried this when we visited the Arctic Circle two years ago. It's become our tradition when we go stargazing now: James with his whisky, me with my mint vodka.

"Do you remember that trip to Finland?" I ask. "When we saw the Perseid meteor shower?"

"I do." James heads back towards me. "I wonder how many meteors we saw that night. One, two hundred? We ate reindeer."

"I'd forgotten about the Rudolph steaks."

James sits beside me, on the rug we've laid down in a gap between the gorse bushes. "Where's this planet, then?"

"I've lost it."

The fleece of James's collar brushes my neck. "You'll find it, sweetheart."

I could suggest we take our clothes off, right here and now, in the freezing January night. We could get horny and hypothermic.

"Shouldn't have taken my eyes off it." I'm not sure why my brain makes me say this. Why it doesn't suggest sex.

"I'm pleased with these." James taps the binoculars. He recently inherited them from his great-grandfather. A relic, originally used on a German U-boat in the Second World War. Last year, we went to Bodmin Moor with a telescope so complicated we spent the entire time gazing at an instruction manual.

"Wait. I've got it." I can't see any of the features, obviously—the craters or polar caps—but I can see enough to make me feel light-headed. Without moving, I ask, "Do you think there's life up there?"

James sniffs. "It's entirely possible there's some bacteria."

"I hope we discover that bacteria in our lifetime."

"Discover it? We'll be living alongside it."

"Do you really think so?"

"Well, there's that competition. Where the prize is to go and live on Mars."

"Liar." I elbow James in the ribs.

"I'm serious. Heard a thing about it on the radio. The winners are flying out there in a few years—but the catch is that they can never come back."

"Why not?"

"Money. Technology. Sensationalism."

I blink, trying to get Mars back into focus, wondering how it might feel to call that place home.

"James," I say, with an urgency that surprises me. "Don't you think it might be fun to enter?" I unscrew the lid of my vodka. "We could end up living on Mars together! It'd be so romantic."

"Ha," James responds. "I'm not sure that's my idea of romance."

I screw the lid back on my bottle, suddenly not thirsty. "Yeah. I was just kidding."

"We should head back to Falmouth soon," James yawns. "Before Bolster eats us for breakfast."

Legend has it that Bolster was a murderous giant from these parts. One day, he fell in love with a young woman called Agnes. Agnes was aware of Bolster's cruel nature and decided to play a trick on him. She told him to prove his affection for her by filling a hole in the clifftops with his blood. What Bolster didn't know was that the hole had a crack in it, which ran all the way down to the sea. He took a knife and sliced open his veins, spilling his vital fluids into the unfillable chasm until, finally, he bled out.

"Solvig? Are you ready to go?"

"I will be," I say. "Very soon." I take one last look at the planet, then pass James the binoculars. "Go on. It beats spiders."

As James scans the sky, I can feel the blood draining out of me, flowing towards that red dot in the sky, then spilling out into the darkness.

2

"Welcome to Go Ape," says the man behind the desk. "How many are in your party?"

"Oh," I tell him, "it's just me. I'm going ape alone."

The man studies my booking reference. "That's one gorilla, then."

"Pardon?"

"You're a gorilla. Baboons are under fifteen. Gorillas are sixteen and over."

I look at the primates in the queue behind me. "I'm scouting out the place for a work event," I say. "That's why I'm here on my own. To check if it's suitable." I scratch my nose. "For my colleagues."

The man behind the desk looks neither sceptical nor interested. "Fill in this paperwork," he says, handing me a clipboard, "then we'll get you kitted out."

I head to a bench running along one side of the cabin, listening to the crinkle of my waterproof trousers as I sit. I tick the "no" box for every question on my medical history. It feels good to let a stranger know I'm in peak condition. I sign the form with a flourish and then hand it back.

The man behind the desk barely looks at it. "You're in the yellow group, Ms. Dean. Wait by that door to collect your equipment."

I loiter by the closed door, wondering who'll be in my group. I'm not sure how Go Ape works—whether it's a competitive thing. I feel competitive.

I switch on my phone and go to Safari, to look at a site that I've visited several times since James and I went stargazing last week. On the home page is a big red button that says: "Join the Mars Project." For the umpteenth time, I press it.

The rules of the competition are simple: fill in the entry form, tick a box saying that you understand that if you're chosen for the mission, you'll never return to Earth, and then wait. There will be interviews, activities, and even some kind of online vote to select the crew.

I can't believe there's nothing in the eligibility criteria that excludes *me* from entering something like this. There are certain guidelines, like: "In reasonable health . . . Good-natured individual . . . Fast learner . . ." But everyone in this hut right now would probably describe themselves in those terms. Still, it makes you think.

"Morning, lads and lasses!" says a woman emerging from behind the door. "Can all the gorillas come forward, please? You need to pick up your harnesses."

I'm first in the queue. I look back at the other gorillas, casting them a quick, hopefully not-too-smug smile. Most are too busy communicating with their baboons to notice me.

"Small, medium, or large, pet?" asks the woman. Behind her is a storeroom full of belts and buckles.

"Large," I say, straightening my spine and revealing my full six feet to her.

She stares at me. "Reckon you're only a medium, sweetheart." She hands me a harness. "All about your waist circumference, see." She motions to the person behind me. "Are you two together?"

"No," I tell her. "I'm here on my own. Scouting out the place for a work event."

"Pop it on over there, please."

I'm going to be honest for the rest of the day. Why shouldn't a grown woman attend Go Ape on her own? I've been wanting to come here for ages, but James has always called it a "glorified kids' playground," and it's definitely not Anouk's sort of thing. Besides, she's been more or less off the radar since becoming a mum. With James at work, and nothing to do on this drizzly day, I jumped in the car and drove here by myself. No shame in that.

I go back to the bench and put on my equipment.

"Tricky," laughs a woman in an orange anorak beside me, as her harness falls to the floor. She snorts with amusement. I move to the other end of the bench.

"Hi, team." A guy of about my age approaches us, with a ginger beard and a can-do attitude. He's wearing a black puffer jacket with the company logo on it, and his harness is already attached. "My name's Matty, and I'll be taking you on your Treetop Adventure today."

Matty checks our harnesses and talks us through some basic safety stuff, then leads us out into the forest. I walk directly behind him, hoping that he'll make conversation with me. He merely looks back every now and then to check that we're all present. Eight gorillas, five baboons, and two hard-to-tells.

I listen to the squelch of my boots in the mud. You wouldn't know that we're so near to Exeter. I love being in places where all you can see is nature in every direction. Here, we're surrounded by trees and hills. It's a wilderness of sorts.

Matty comes to a stop and does an about-turn. "Who's ready for some fun?" he asks, pointing to a rope ladder. The rope ladder is not much taller than I am. "It's time to practise climbing!"

As Matty explains the colour-coding system and how to deal with a fear of heights, I get out my phone and take a surreptitious look.

"If you want to win this competition," it says on the Mars Project site, "you're going to need to be able to fly into the face of danger."

I wonder what sort of training you'd need to do to go to Mars. Would rope ladders be involved? Probably not, but you've got to start somewhere. I put my phone away and concentrate on what Matty's saying.

Ten minutes later, we get to the zip wires, and I glide weightlessly through the air, with nothing but a small hook to keep me anchored. I feel ready for anything.

3

"I've discovered my passion," James announces, as we walk along Gyllyngvase Beach.

We're throwing an inflatable red ball back and forth. It was lying on the sand this morning, a gift from the ocean.

"Your passion?" I hold on to the ball for a moment.

"It's sourdough," says James. "I'm going to make a starter culture and keep it going for years. I'm going to eat sourdough from the same starter when I'm a hundred."

Aside from the red ball, other things that have washed up on the beach recently include: three dolphin carcasses, a Lego pirate, and innumerable shards of coloured glass. Flotsam and jetsam. Frothy words, making an ocean in the mouth. They're types of marine debris. *Flotsam* is normally the result of a shipwreck. It floats on the water after an accidental spillage. *Jetsam* has been thrown into the water intentionally. Most likely it was chucked over the side of a sinking ship to lighten the load. People always forget about lagan and derelict. *Lagan* is attached to a buoy so that the owner can find it again. *Derelict* sinks to the seafloor.

"Solvig?" James asks. "What do you think? About my bread idea?"

"Eating sourdough. When you're a hundred. Yum." I throw the ball back. My arms are still aching from Go Ape.

The flotsam and jetsam of a relationship. It sounds like a nice phrase, but that would make the relationship a relationship *wreck*. That's not the way I see me and James. Better to say that I have my own flotsam and jetsam. Things that have fallen away by accident, and things that I threw overboard, abandoned to lighten the load, many years ago. Things that float to the surface when the cracks appear.

This time, I miss the ball. As I pick it up, James points at the sand.

"Look, a sea raft," he says.

Is that another new tattoo on his wrist? Looks like an ouroboros. Tail eater. Constantly leaving, constantly returning.

"That's unusual," he muses. "It's a by-the-wind sailor. From the *Porpitidae* family."

It's a glutinous disc of cobalt blue. Size of a Ritz cracker. There's a flap of clear gel on top.

"That's the sail," James says. "It blows wherever the wind takes it."

"A life of freedom," I respond.

James shakes his head. "Completely at the mercy of the elements. A kind of prison."

I kneel down, as if to inspect the creature. I find myself inspecting my trainers instead. The sole is peeling away from the left shoe.

"Don't touch it," James warns, "because of the nematocysts. Neat, aren't they? Living at the intersection between air and water. Sails on top, polyps underneath. Organisms that live in and out of water at the same time are—"

"Amphibians."

"No. Pleuston." James buys nature books with Latin words in them. He watches programmes narrated by David Attenborough and Chris Packham. At work, he spends his days etching marine life onto people's skin: a squid on the biceps, a koi carp on the thigh, a stingray on the sacrum. This fetishisation of the sea. *Thalassophilia*, as it's known. Try spending ten hours on the seabed, people, I always think, and then tell me about your love of the velvet dogfish.

James has already moved on. "I'm going to capture the wild yeast in the environment." He's gesticulating a lot. I think he's plucking imaginary yeast particles from the air. "I'm going to use it to naturally ferment my bread. Good, eh?"

We trudge towards Gylly Beach Café to warm up. Before we go in, James hands the ball to a little girl in frog-shaped wellington boots. Then he sits with his back to the window, so that I get a view of the sea.

"I can't believe this is our last day together," he says, once our drinks have arrived.

"It's only for a month," I tell him. "It'll whizz by."

"I wanted to do something special. I wish I didn't have to work this afternoon."

I lift my cup to my lips and take a sip of black coffee. "This is special."

We've been together for nearly three years. Every time I go it's the same. James is a romantic. But he wouldn't be in love with me if I were the sort of person who didn't go away regularly. And I wouldn't love him if I stayed. That's how this works: I get time to myself, and James gets a break from my dark moods before they grow unbearable.

"I'll make it up to you later," he says, taking his cup and gently nudging mine.

"A normal night in will be fine. I like our normal nights."

Just then, a plate smashes beyond the swinging doors, in the kitchen. A crackle of jealousy runs through me as I imagine the waiter sweeping up broken crockery.

James studies me. "It's happening again, isn't it?"

It feels like my bones are being crushed. I nod.

"You get like this every time now," James says, "right before you leave. I'm worried that your job is putting too much strain on you. I mean, you went to Go Ape the other day. You're spiralling." He smiles with his mouth but not his eyes.

James is wrong. My work isn't stressful—it's the opposite. I love it. I live for it. The longer I go without it, the more frustrated I get. After an idle week or two, a voice will pipe up. *What are you doing with your life, Solvig? Is this it? Do you merely exist to drink Americanos and eat avocados and talk about the weather?* Once the voice grows deafening, that's when the physical pain starts. Sore throats. Migraines. Indigestion. The only cure is to get back to the grindstone.

Unfortunately, legally, I have to take at least a month off between jobs. And even if I could go back sooner, chances are there'd be no work for me. I can go half a year between assignments. Poor weather conditions, seasonal demands, plans changing at the last minute . . . if I didn't love what I do so much, it'd be my worst nightmare.

Tomorrow I'm flying to Aberdeen. I'll enter a pressurised chamber on board a ship on the North Sea. This will be my home for a month. Every day, I'll climb out of a hatch in the chamber into a diving bell and plunge to a depth of around 130 metres. The proper name for my job is *saturation diving*. Saturation diving is my medicine. Hopefully, once I get back to it, I'll stop obsessing over the Mars Project.

"I wonder if it'll rain today," I say.

The waiter heads out of the kitchen holding our breakfasts: full Cornish for James, waffles with winter berries for me.

James starts to eat. As I glance at his throat, which is one of the only places—save his face—that isn't tattooed, I see a pulse beneath his skin. I feel the need to touch my own neck, first on one side, then the other. I don't think I have OCD. That sounds too definite and interesting for what I've got. I've got a gnawing need for bodily symmetry. I try to ensure both eyelids shut with equal pressure. If I press one knee, I prod the other. When I look at James's tattoo sleeves, I wish I could pull the peonies on the right arm down a few centimetres, to make them even with the skulls on the left. However, the fact that James is an amputee and is missing his lower left leg has never bothered me.

"Aren't you hungry?" James asks. His mouth is full of hog's pudding: pork, oatmeal, pearl barley.

I'd been planning to do a twenty-mile run after this. But when James ordered the full Cornish, I knew I'd offend him if I didn't order something extravagant. I pick up my knife and fork.

James reaches across the table for my hand. I let him take it, but my fist remains clenched, still holding my cutlery.

"Solvig," he says. "I wanted today to be special for a reason." He's staring at the salt shaker as insistently as if it were my eyes. "I don't know if it's the right time to bring this up. You know what I'm like. I find it hard to keep things in."

He's so porous, everything cascades out of him.

"Seriously, if you're not up for it, then say," he continues. "I was thinking, though, that since we're so settled now—we've got the house and the dog and our careers—that it might be nice, or even . . . amazing . . . to start, well . . ."

My chest tightens.

James squeezes my hand. "Start trying for a baby."

I focus on the condensation running down the window.

James keeps talking. He talks about how he wants to do some fence repairs in the front garden, about how he'd love to re-create a nursery he's seen on Pinterest, about how pleased he is that his parents live nearby, and about how fantastic his sourdough is going to taste.

I nod in between mouthfuls of waffle. I nod and eat, nod and eat. I know how lucky I am. I'm so lucky to be here, in my idyllic hometown, with my kind and handsome boyfriend. Everything is perfect between us. We have all the necessary prerequisites to create human life. Why wouldn't I want to start trying for a family? Why wouldn't I want that?

•

After James heads to work, I'm desperate to run and run, as far as I can possibly go. Running on a full stomach is a bad idea, so I'm compromising and only doing ten miles.

This baby thing has thrown me into disarray. Certainly, I've acknowledged that one day, I might want to grow a child inside my body. But even though I'm the grand old age of thirty-six, I've never stopped to think that "one day" might be today. And if it's not today, then how much time have I got left?

As I run along the seafront, I weigh up the pros and cons. Pros: babies make you feel fulfilled. Cons: babies stop you from feeling fulfilled.

What if there are other things I want to do with my life, big things, things I couldn't possibly do with children?

I look up at Pendennis Point. Then I slow down, catching my breath. My stomach is in knots. I hurry down some stone steps leading off the pavement. They take me onto the beach. I hurry to the water, then hunch over, bent double, emptying my guts into the sea. A mass of burgundy-coloured winter berries floats, half-digested, on the surface. Flotsam.

I wipe my mouth and lie back on the sand, squinting. The sky is blank. I extend my arms and reach out for it.

4

A hot shower makes everything better. That's what my dad always says. But as I emerge from the bathroom, wrapped in a fluffy towel, it's not my dad I'm thinking of—it's my mum.

She died two months before my third birthday. I don't remember her. I don't know if I called her Mum or Mummy or Elaine. I don't know what her voice sounded like, or what she liked to eat for breakfast. I do know that it was my mum who chose a Scandinavian name for me. She was into *hygge* long before it was fashionable; said my name reminded her of a bowl of split pea soup. That's one of the only things she wrote in my baby book. My mum was a genius and didn't have time for filling in books for babies.

I head into the spare room, leaving a trail of wet footprints on the floorboards. The shelves in here are crammed mostly with James's stuff: tattoo guns, inks, needles, machine tips. We once had a house party where James gave free tattoos to his friends all night. There are people living all over Cornwall who've been forever changed by that party. Like Kensa, who works at the bike shop and has a top hat on his middle finger. Or Polly, who teaches at the university and sports "wanderlust" on her clavicle. I didn't get a tattoo that night, of course. The permanence frightens me.

I take a Quality Street tin off the bottom shelf. This is mine. I take off the tin's rusty lid and sift through the old photographs inside. There's me winning the long jump at school; me dressed as Fred Flintstone for Halloween; me and Dad on a canal boat, both gripping enamel mugs. I can't remember the days these pictures were taken, but I know the photographs so well that they feel like memories. When I see the canal boat photo, for instance, I think about the taste of hot cocoa. It's possible that we were actually drinking tea.

At the bottom of the pile, there are six pictures that I know even better than any of the others:

1. Mum is a baby, trying to eat her christening gown.
2. Mum is a teenager, sitting on a bed with two girls and a boy, wearing bell-bottoms, laughing.
3. Mum is lying on a sun lounger next to a swimming pool, wearing a bikini. The photograph is taken from above, presumably from a hotel balcony. My mum looks as though she's sleeping peacefully.
4. Mum is blinking, holding hands with my dad in front of a sparsely decorated Christmas tree. Mum is at least six centimetres taller than Dad. Dad's pupils are glowing red.
5. Mum is in the house my dad still lives in, lying on the sofa he still sits on. I am on the sofa too. We are staring

at something off-camera, probably the television. There
are two cans of beer on the coffee table.

6. Mum is sitting in front of an IBM computer, wearing
a brown smock. I, the photographer, am looking up
at Mum at a wonky angle, cutting her head out of the
picture. There's a bottle of Smirnoff on her desk.

I know my mother was a genius because of the things my dad
has told me. About how she used to spend fifteen hours a day
at her desk, and even then, she would wake up three or four
times a night, scribbling notes on a pad beside the bed. I wonder how someone so focused on her high-flying career in IT
felt about having me. Is it a coincidence that the photographs
I'm in also have alcohol in them? Or was her heavy drinking by
the end a way of trying to calm her busy mind?

I share Mum's passion for work. And being a saturation
diver doesn't exactly mesh with motherhood. Working away
from home for big chunks of time. Risking my health—my
life, even. Also, I'm self-employed. That means no maternity
leave. No contract. If I choose to have a baby, I need to prepare
myself for the possibility that I may never do the job I love
again.

My best friend, Anouk, is a practising physiotherapist. We
haven't discussed how she feels about her work-life balance
since she adopted Nike. She's never complained, so I've always
assumed it's going just fine.

I send a text message asking if I can come over. By the time
I've put the pictures of my mother back in the tin, I've had a
reply. She says: *Yes. Please. Now.*

I'm off to see my Mum Friend, I think experimentally, as I pull on a pair of tracksuit bottoms. *She's a mum, I'm a mum, we're Mum Friends.* I put on a faded mauve sweatshirt I've had for years. The kind of thing a mum would wear.

"Where's my baby?" I call in a silly voice as I walk downstairs. My seven-year-old Irish wolfhound, Cola, hobbles into the hallway. In human years, he is roughly the same age as Jeremy Irons.

"Fancy a peregrination, old man?" I give his grey muzzle a stroke.

Two years ago, when we got Cola from the shelter, he would get so excited at the word "walk" that he'd wee on the carpet. We started saying "stroll" instead, but he quickly cottoned on, so now I make full use of the thesaurus.

I attach Cola's lead to his collar and put on my parka, and we leave the house.

As we walk, I look across Penryn River. The boats are pointing north today, towards Flushing. I love the way they line up depending on the swell of the tide. There isn't a day goes by that I don't feel glad to live here.

I take a right up Symons Hill, which I remind myself to go up extra slowly. Cola stops occasionally and looks up at me with doleful eyes, then shuffles on.

"Good boy, Cola."

Some people have already put their bins out ready for tomorrow. The most conscientious have blankets and ropes keeping their rubbish out of reach of greedy birds. The seagulls here are fat and ferocious. It doesn't matter how posh your house is, or how delightful its shade of coastal blue, every exterior is splattered with guano.

"Soffig!" a little voice cries out, accompanied by some en-
thusiastic waving. Farther up the hill, on Jubilee Road, is Nike.
It must be at least six weeks since I was last at Anouk's. I feel
honoured that he remembers me.

"Hoy there," calls Anouk, letting go of Nike's hand.

"Look what I made, Soffig!" Nike runs towards me. He's
wearing a navy sweatshirt with a red collar poking out, and
he's carrying an A3 poster with black and green clumps stuck
all over it. He pants exaggeratedly, hands me the poster, and
then bends down and almost pokes Cola in the eye. "Hello,
Mr. Coca-Cola."

I study Nike's poster, trying to identify the blobs. "It's
lovely."

"His class went beachcombing," Anouk explains, a few
steps away from me now. "Nike's picture is called *Stupid Fish*,
isn't it, doodle?"

Nike is too busy stroking Cola to respond. I hand him
Cola's lead. "Remember how I showed you to do it last time?
That's it, let him lead you."

Nike nods solemnly, as if he's been given the most important job in the world. As we walk up Beacon Road, Anouk and
I hang back a little.

"How's he settling in?" I ask quietly.

Anouk hasn't told me why Nike was placed for adoption,
and I've never asked, even though I'm dying to know. Would
knowing help me understand Nike or Anouk better? I doubt it.
It's voyeurism, plain and simple.

"Pretty good," she says. "They've only been back at school
for a week, but he seems much happier this term."

Nike is five. He's been living with Anouk for almost a year, but she only officially adopted him in August. His foster family was in Plymouth, and relocating was tough on him. The adoption agency thought the quietness of Falmouth would do him good.

Nike has definitely come out of his shell since he first came to Anouk. I remember that first week, when Nike hid behind the sofa, swearing. Anouk texted me every day with messages full of capital letters. Gradually, the messages subsided, and I presumed, perhaps incorrectly, that she wanted some space.

"And how about you?" I ask. "How are you getting on?" I try not to ask this in a way that sounds like I'm testing her. Really, though, I am. Anouk is my litmus test. If she's struggling with motherhood, then I've got no chance.

Anouk laughs, patting me on the shoulder. "I'm fine. Frazzled. Discombobulated. But fine."

I know appearances can be deceiving, but Anouk doesn't seem frazzled. She's dressed in dungarees and a mustard chenille jumper. She has a polka-dot scarf wrapped around her head, red lipstick on, and looks about a hundred times as cool as I've ever done.

I want to ask her if having a kid is worth it. Does she feel sure that she made the right decision? Instead, I say: "You're doing great."

Anouk laughs again, then narrows her eyes. "You're off tomorrow, aren't you? Don't worry, I'm not going through another psychic phase. James mentioned it." Anouk has known James for longer than she's known me. Sometimes I forget that they're friends too, that they talk to each other when I'm not there.

Anouk looks like she's about to say something else, then stops. When we reach her place, a yellow-doored end-of-terrace with two palm trees in the front garden, she pats Nike on the back. "Why don't you go around the back and play in the garden with Cola, doodle?"

"Okay, pukey Anouky." Nike sticks out his tongue.

I sit on the sofa while Anouk makes tea. The living room has a nautical theme: blue and white furniture, shells on the mantelpiece, a framed print of a life preserver on the wall. A lot of Cornish homes are decorated like this. The main difference between Anouk's front room and most of the others around here is the statue of Ganesha next to the television.

Anouk brings in the teas and sits beside me. "I'm glad you got in touch," she says, an unfamiliar vulnerability in her voice. She reaches into her pocket and pulls out a smooth green pebble. "I've been carrying this around with me lately, but I'd like you to have it now." She passes it to me. "It's malachite. For protection."

Anouk used to work in a crystal shop in Camborne, near the Giant's Quoit: a mysterious megalithic tomb. She took several boxes of stock home with her when the shop closed down, and she would jokingly administer "stones for yer bones" when we met up. "This one will cure your cold," she'd say, or, "This one will stop you and James arguing over the remote." Anouk is not laughing now.

"You know I'm proud of you, girl," she says, looking at the carpet. "But be careful, okay?"

I frown. Has James told her he wants to try for a baby?

"I saw this documentary a couple of nights ago," she says. "The guy on it, a diver, he made one tiny mistake. He opened a valve at the wrong time, and the whole chamber blew up. I don't want you to explode, Solvig."

Anouk must be talking about the Byford Dolphin case. When the chamber exploded, one of the divers was propelled through a sixty-centimetre opening. Fragments of his body were found ten metres away. "It was one of the tenders outside the chamber who made the mistake," I tell her. "Not a diver."

Anouk scowls.

"You big dafty," I say, giving her arm a squeeze. I mean, really, I'm not going to come out and say it, but there's no way a lump of rock is going to save me. It's like the old saying goes: if it's your time to be forced through a sixty-centimetre opening, it's your time to be forced through a sixty-centimetre opening. Strange to hear Anouk worrying like that, though. She used to call my job "badass."

I pick up my cup of tea. "Anyway, how's *your* work going?"

"It's fine," she says. "I mean, it's awful. Exhausting. Brilliant."

"Anouk," I begin.

Anouk looks at me. I notice the dark, puffy skin under her eyes. I think about how she's been carrying a pebble in her pocket for protection.

"Listen," I tell her. "If you ever need a night off, and you want me to babysit, let me know. I'd be happy to look after Nike."

Anouk bites down on her lower lip. "Thank you, Solvig. By the way, you'll know when danger is coming, because the stone will shatter. If that happens: watch out."

•

"Good run earlier?" James calls.

I take off Cola's lead, then go into the kitchen and see James shredding celeriac. He's been talking about this recipe for days. Crispy catfish with black-eyed peas and Southern-style slaw. The key to this meal, he says, is coating the fish with cornflakes instead of breadcrumbs. It sounds . . . gross.

"My run was great, thanks," I lie.

I look in the fridge at the selection of half-drunk reds and whites. I take a red and pour it into two glasses without bothering to try any, then put a glass on the counter next to James.

"Cheers," he says.

"Bottoms up," I reply.

I wonder if we're going to keep carrying on as though the conversation earlier never happened. Maybe it's my responsibility to bring it up first. James said I could take my time to think about it. What would happen if I thought about it for a year? Ten years? I put on my best smile. "Want some help?"

"No need." James grabs my waist. His breath is vegetal. James once showed me a YouTube video of a whisky taster who advised viewers to develop their palates by tasting unusual things. He recommended starting with a fresh bay leaf. I had a pack of dried leaves in the cupboard, and they were so sharp they sliced my tongue.

I politely extricate myself from James's grip and put out food and medication for Cola, then collapse on the sofa. Being on the verge of leaving really makes me appreciate what I've got here. We might not have cornicing, ceiling roses, or fancy banisters like the homes facing the sea have, but our house—which looks over the harbour—is cosy, with big windows. The winter can be a pain, though. The house gets damp and freezing, and once it's dark, all you can see out of the windows is yourself.

My reflection is just starting to appear in the window now. I can see James's too. I'm embarrassed by how we look together. The same height, both with blond hair and blue eyes. James's hair is long and mine is short. Does that help? Not really. I once bought some dye, but I never used it.

"I picked up a couple of books for you on my way home," James says, nodding at the coffee table.

I get a lot of reading done on my dives. Problem is, the library lends books for only three weeks, so I have to buy them. Inevitably, I end up taking a weird mix of whatever secondhand books this seaside town has to offer. Fortunately, the wintertime choice is generally more interesting than the summer. Come July and August, the shops are brimming with discarded tourist reads. That's how I ended up with three books on the history of fascism in November, whereas in August, it was seven romcoms by Marian Keyes.

I look at the books on the table: a crime novel and a book of Cornish folktales.

"I had a flick through," James says. "Some of the folktales look more disturbing than the thriller."

I laugh. "Thanks. You really don't need to make such a fuss. It's my job."

"I'm worried about you," James says, stirring the black-eyed peas. "This—I don't know what it is—depression, or whatever you're feeling." He carefully places two fillets into a sizzling pan. "You don't have to do it, you know. We can find something else. Some of those inland diving jobs are—"

"Love you," I say, getting up from the sofa and going to give him a kiss. My lips miss and hit the corner of his mouth.

•

"Soul food." James puts a plate in front of me.

There's a vase of snowdrops on the table and Van Morrison is singing about the fires of spring on the record player.

"Turns out breakfast cereal and fish are a great pairing," I say, after taking a small bite.

James sighs. There are dark circles under his eyes. "Needs more spice."

I put down my fork. "How was work, love?"

"The customer wanted a jellyfish at the bottom of his back. He said he wanted it to literally glow . . . I'll show you the crime scene later." "Crime scene" is what we jokingly call the photos James takes straight after he's done a tattoo, when the customer's skin is raw and beads of blood are bubbling up out of the puncture wounds. I love those pictures; James is normally so gentle that it excites me to see evidence of his brutality.

"James," I say. "I'm definitely thinking about it."

I'm not lying. I think about it over the rest of dinner, and I think about it while we watch *Alien* on the sofa. I think about it when the creature bursts out of the man's stomach, and I think about it while I load the dishwasher, and I think about it while I brush my teeth, and I think about it when we turn off the lights, and then, under the covers, in complete darkness, in the tiniest voice, I whisper: "Yes, let's do it. Let's make a baby."

5

How are you ever supposed to know what you want?

I remember being in the garage with my dad when I was a kid, about ten. My aunt Marie popped in and said, "I'm off to the shops, ducky. Want to come?"

Dad was in the middle of welding a table, and I was meant to be helping out. Helping out involved handing tools to Dad when he needed them, and it was a sacred job. My father was a craftsman and an artist. He welded everything from massive yard installations to miniature model cars. I loved to watch him work.

But I also loved going to the shops.

"Are you going to the Entertainer?" I asked. I was on the lookout for a new onionskin or peewee to add to my marble collection.

Aunt Marie smiled. "I think we can manage that." My dad's older sister lived with us for a few years after Mum died. I was grateful to have her around, but then she died too. An infected hip replacement.

"Okay," I said. "I'll come with you." I skipped down the street until I reached next door's hydrangea bush; then I froze. "Gah! I'm going back."

I ran back inside and handed Dad a length of steel tubing. And then I thought about all the marbles I might never own, and I ran outside again. Aunt Marie was at the lamppost on the corner.

"Hurry up then, child," she called, shaking her head.

"No!" I shouted, realising it was my dad I wanted to be with after all. I ran back to the garage, and instantly regretted it. I rushed out, panting, but Aunt Marie was too far away to catch up.

I cried too much to see the table being finished.

Now I've learnt the secret to making decisions. It's all about diving in. Am I hungry? I'll eat a sandwich to find out. Am I tired yet? I'll go to bed and see. Do I want a baby? I don't know. Let's have unprotected sex and see how it feels.

•

"I Want to Break Free" by Queen plays on my phone at 5:30 a.m. It's been my alarm for years. I normally press snooze around the time Freddie Mercury announces that he's fallen in love, but today I don't. I don't check my emails, I don't jump out of bed, and I don't take my birth control pill. Freddie Mercury repeats the phrase "I want" four times in a row.

I begin to stroke different parts of my boyfriend. Collarbone. Sternum. Hips. I can feel the ridges of tattoos on his skin. I try to trace shapes with my fingertips, but it's impossible.

I know what I'm touching anyway: Poseidon; a wolf with a woman's face coming out of its mouth; a sword piercing a peach.

"Don't go." James rolls over and pulls me in close.

"I'm not going anywhere," I say. "At least, not right now."

6

Whenever I'm in Aberdeen, I'm about to start a job or I've just finished one. It's a portal between worlds.

I lived in Scotland for a few years, back when I was doing my training. I got my offshore qualifications in Argyll, then my saturation certificate in Fort William. The whole lot cost twenty grand. Dad was furious when he found out how I'd blown Mum's inheritance. He thought diving was another of my phases. Since studying construction at college, I'd tried plastering, carpentry, brickwork, and welding. I was working as a welder fabricator at the time, and even though my plan was to keep welding, but to do it underwater instead of on land, my dad freaked out. "If you want to weld, Sol, you want to weld," he told me. "You don't need water to make it more extreme or whatever." But he soon saw how much those first diving trips changed me. For the first time in my life, I stopped trying to run away, and I started running towards something.

I ended up living in Glasgow, because that's where my first job was. Vessel repair work—nothing fancy, but it took months. Before I knew it, I owned things: saucepans, a coffee table, all the trappings of modern life. Ideally, I'd have lived on the water. The curse of the *Flying Dutchman* used to sound like heaven to me: endlessly drifting, never docking. As I've grown older, I've become more accustomed to saucepans. Mooring safely in a harbour from time to time is not such a bad thing. It's just a case of dropping your anchor in the right place.

I call James outside the airport to let him know I've arrived safely. We don't mention what happened this morning. Instead, we talk about what we're having for lunch. "I'm experimenting with a keto recipe," James says. "You?"

"Panini from Costa."

When I hang up, I feel a pang of regret. Why didn't we talk about it? Are we embarrassed? Is it unlucky? Like one of those old maritime superstitions, where you're not supposed to say certain words at sea. Words like *goodbye* and *drown*, because if you speak them aloud, you're inviting disaster.

I stand in the taxi queue, breathing in the cold air, then breathing out the steam from inside my lungs. I like exhaling steam. It makes me feel like a machine. When I'm in the diving chamber, I'm no longer human. I'm a cog.

•

Our diving support vessel is called the *Seawell*. Its belly is full of tubes, gases, valves: stuff that will keep us alive for the next month. And if something goes wrong, it's stuff that could kill us too.

A lot of people think that my job involves living on the seafloor for a month at a time. It doesn't. I'll be right here, on board the ship, in a chamber that's not much bigger than a garden shed. The three separate compartments—for living, sanitation, and sleep—take up little more than ten square metres in total. It's strange to think that while we're locked in our cramped metal enclosure, dozens of other workers are all around us, so close that if the walls weren't there we'd be able to reach out and touch them.

Once you're in the chamber, of course, you don't really think about that. You forget that anything exists beyond that which you can see. You sort of have to.

Four of the other divers on my team are already in the ship's belly, performing safety checks.

"Just warning you guys that I have not had a shit in three days," says Eryk. He's Polish, with a badly drawn paw-print tattoo on one side of his bald head.

Rich throws a wellington boot at him. I've never dived with Rich—he's new to saturation—but he seems to be fitting in.

Dale zips up his rucksack and looks over his shoulder. "Where's that lazy bugger Tai got to, eh? He'd better leave enough time for all his checks." Dale has been doing this since the seventies. Back then, half a dozen divers died every year. Though he won't go into the details, I know he had to bring up the dismembered head of a fellow diver on one occasion. When Dale has advice for us, we tend to listen.

"He's around," Cal says. Cal is a man of few words.

Eryk switches his headlamp on and off a couple of times. "If he doesn't come down soon, I'm nicking his stinger suit."

"You'll never fit in it, you fat bastard," replies Dale.

The banter is all part of a highly choreographed routine. Behind every joke is a huge amount of subtext: I am prepared for this dive. I am comfortable around you. I will make the next twenty-eight days easy for you. I would save your life if you were in peril.

"Still doing your checks, people? I finished ages ago." Tai has just appeared, clutching six white straws.

We all stop what we're doing.

"This is gonna be the fifth dive in a row I get the top bunk, guys, I'm telling you," says Eryk. He picks a short straw out of Tai's palm and everyone laughs. "Fuck's sake, man."

The top bunks are more cramped than the bottom ones. Plus, you worry about waking people up every time you climb up or down, and your stuff keeps falling out onto the metal grate.

"Let's have a go," I say, stepping forwards. "I'm gonna pick one while the odds are in my favour." I flex my hands as if preparing to play the piano, and then slowly draw out a long white straw. "Boom." I speak like this when I'm diving. "Gonna." "Boom." When you spend so much time in such close quarters with one another, language, like just about everything else, is contagious.

"Lucky, Deano, lucky," says Rich. Most of the guys here call me Deano, because of my surname. Or they call me "lad," "mate," or "pal." Doesn't bother me. If they're afraid of my femaleness, that's not my problem. Besides, there are hardly any women who do this job. In fact, the first time I ever heard of sat diving was on a BBC series about extreme jobs called *Real*

Men. I knew as soon as I saw it that I wanted to be a Real Man. And being a Real Man makes me feel like more of a Real Woman than ever before.

Once the bunks are decided, and we've made sure that our gear is watertight, airtight, and in full working order, we head for the chamber. As we wait outside the small circular hatch, we pat each other on the back. We hum under our breath.

Then the hatch opens, and the joking resumes.

"What's up, Solvig?" Tai asks, as we wait our turn to climb in. Tai is one of the only people here who use my first name. He learnt to dive in Nigeria. The fish are stunning there, he says, but you have to watch out for the groupers. He once told me a story about a diver who exited a diving bell and went foot-first into a grouper's gaping mouth.

"I'm good, thanks, Tai," I say. "You?"

He shrugs. "Can't complain."

Last time we were on a dive, Tai told me his mother had just been diagnosed with pancreatic cancer, but now doesn't seem like the time to ask after her. Bringing that sort of baggage in with us feels wrong.

I'm the last diver to enter the chamber, and I pause to take a deep breath before climbing in. Moments later, the hatch is closed behind me.

•

It takes about eighty minutes for the air pressure to reach that of the bottom of the North Sea. During blowdown, the temperature rises to over thirty degrees Celsius. The guys sort out their bunks while I sit sweating in front of the camera for dive control.

I flip open my Head & Shoulders and unscrew my Colgate. Even the tiniest air pocket can be unsafe. If your tooth has a cavity, for example, it could rupture during compression. I've seen a guy's crown get blown off, taking the whole tooth—and a big chunk of his gum—with it.

If you get ill while you're in here, you can't just nip out of the chamber. Doesn't matter if you're having a heart attack or a stroke or you're gushing with blood. If you decompress too quickly, your body will fill with bubbles. And if the bubbles reach your brain, you're screwed. It takes five and a half days to decompress safely. Even if there's an emergency on the ship. Even if the whole place is burning down around you.

Back at the airport drugstore, I hurriedly bought a pack of prenatal vitamins. They've got folic acid, vitamin D, and some other scientific-sounding stuff in them: l-arginine, n-acetyl cysteine, inositol. The chemicals needed to build healthy human beings, I guess. I open the pack while it's still in my bag and check there's nothing in it that could explode. I leave it hidden among knives and spanners.

"Deano?" someone calls. It gets harder to recognise people's voices as the air pressure increases. We're being fed a gas called heliox, which is a mixture of helium and oxygen. The helium is used as a substitute for nitrogen, which does bad things to the central nervous system at high pressure. The unfortunate side effect of it is that we speak like chipmunks for the entire month.

"Yeah?" I call out. "Whaddya want?" It's the first time I've heard myself like this in four months and I can't help sniggering. It's good to be back.

•

I've been lying on my bunk reading Cornish folktales for half an hour. My favourite story so far is about a fisherman who bravely ventures out in stormy midwinter seas and returns to his village with a generous haul of pilchards. The villagers bake the entire catch into a dish they call stargazy pie, because all the fish heads poke skywards. That image seems strangely romantic to me.

I also read about the ancient site of Mên-an-Tol, where there are three large rocks: two vertical pillars and a hollow circle in the middle, spelling out "101." The legend goes that if a woman climbs through the circle backwards on a full moon, she's guaranteed pregnancy. Meanwhile, if children go through the hole naked nine times, they'll be cured of scrofula.

"John Skinner!" shouts Dale from the other chamber. He's a proud cockney, and he definitely hams up the rhyming slang while in saturation. *Fisherman's daughter*: "water." *Barbwired*: "tired." *John Skinner*: "dinner."

I put down my book and hop off my bunk.

"Scrofula," I murmur.

I wonder if my mum would have climbed backwards through a hole in a rock for me. I wonder if she's up there now, in the sky, gazing down.

The others are already at the table. Dale opens the airlock and takes out six containers.

"Two cods," he says, passing them to Tai and Rich. "Steak. That's mine. Cal, Eryk, the pasta. Deano: vindaloo."

A couple of hours ago, we ordered our dinner by ticking a box on a form. Deciding what I want to eat is one of the only decisions I make while I'm down here. The rest of the time I just follow instructions. I find that very relaxing.

I've requested that my curry be made extra spicy. The cooks try their best to keep us happy, but the pressure stops our food from having flavour. Something to do with nasal mucus and food particles.

We watch an old episode of *Cheers* while we eat. Rich is giggling so much he sounds like the laughing sailor at a fairground arcade. The more he laughs, the more he laughs at his own laugh, until Eryk thwacks him on the shoulder with a spoon.

As Cal and Dale settle down to a game of chess, and Eryk and Rich surf the net for GIFs of cats being startled by cucumbers, I head back to my bunk. I open my wallet and find my passport photo of James. The day this was taken, James was still recovering from the norovirus. He looks pale and clammy. We were about to go on holiday to Rome. "You'll have the best *coppa* of your life," James had said, as we booked our flights. At the time, I misheard him and thought he was being flirtatious. Turned out he was talking about cured meat made from a pig's neck muscle.

Tai lies on the bunk next to mine, reading a book about how to chop wood. He's into artisan crafts, a bit like James, but whereas James is into whittling spoons, Tai is into building log cabins. Whereas James is into fermenting a single bottle of gooseberry wine, Tai is into learning how to cultivate a vine-yard. I have to admit, I've thought once or twice about what it might be like to date someone like Tai, and I've come to the conclusion that it'd be exhausting. That's why James and I suit each other so well. We both like limitations. We once made a wheel of cheese that took eight months to mature. We ate it within a week.

Tai and I lie side by side in silence for a while, until our breaths naturally start to synchronise. Eventually, I ask: "How's the book?"

Tai turns to me, eyes wide and moist. "I know what I need to do now."

I smirk. "What? Chop some wood?"

Tai doesn't smile. "I'm going to help to preserve the knowl-edge of the ancient masters for posterity. It's my legacy."

I don't know what Tai's talking about, but I'm unexpectedly moved. "Tai," I say softly. "Do you think that's important? You know, to think about what you're going to leave behind, once you're gone?"

"It's everything," says Tai. "Without wood, we're nothing."

I realise that perhaps we're talking at cross-purposes, but I mentally replace the word "wood" with "ambition," and I put the photo of James back in my wallet.

7

Not long after my mother died, my father began to tell bedtime stories.

Previously, Mum was the storyteller. Dad has kept two of the picture books she used to read to me. The first was *The Very Hungry Caterpillar*. The pages are well thumbed, with a dirty fingerprint on one of the corners, displaying my mother's loops and whorls. The second, *Peace at Last*, is about a bear with insomnia. It's been vandalised to such a degree that only the start of the story remains legible. It reads: "The hour was late." As a girl, when I couldn't sleep, I used to think about my mother reading me that sentence. I created a voice for her, low and soothing. "The hour was late." It helped.

Dad's stories were always made up. There's one I remember more clearly than all the others. He told it to me one summer evening, after an unusually rainy year following my mother's death. That night, instead of coming into my room with tears in his eyes, my dad walked in smiling, holding a silver fan.

"Get ready for a hot one, pup," he said, putting the fan on my desk. He set it so that it swept the room, first blasting me, then blasting him, then making the curtain shiver.

"Let's see," said my dad, clicking his tongue and pulling the sheets up to my chin. I noticed the beads of sweat on his upper lip. His breath smelt of beer. "Right, then. Once upon a time, in Japan, there was this old woman, right?" He wiped his upper lip, but the sweat immediately reappeared.

"How old?"

"Let's say eighty-four. And even though she was over the hill, so to speak, she still swam in the ocean every day, looking for pearls." My dad explained to me that the old woman was an *ama* diver, which means "woman of the sea." Many ama divers keep working their whole lives long. Some regard them as closer to fish than humans. "Hang on a sec, I forgot to tell you the woman's name. It was Chiyo, which means 'forever.'"

"What does my name mean, Daddy?"

"Your name, Sol, means . . . your mum knew. Something about a house."

I stroked my dad's cheek, preemptively wiping away tears. "Tell me about Chiyo."

My father explained to me that ama diving has been around for two thousand years and it's a dying trade. In order to try to preserve her knowledge for future generations, Chiyo went to meet a young girl in the village, to teach her how to dive. "You're a fogey," the girl said with a groan. "I can't see what I could possibly learn from you."

Chiyo stoically set about showing the girl how to check her tools for the dive. My dad had recently watched a TV programme about Japanese divers, and he revelled in telling me the names of some of those tools, but they haven't stayed with me. What I do recall is that at some point, Dad said: "There's a reason the ama divers of Japan are women, Sol. Do you know what it is?"

"Is it because the men don't want to do it?"

"That could be it, pup," he replied, roaring with laughter. "That could be it. But it's also to do with body fat. Women store more fat in their bodies than men, and it keeps them warmer underwater."

When I heard this, my mind began to wander. I knew men and women looked different on the outside. But it was the first time it ever struck me that their insides might be different. The discovery set something off in me, and the colour of that something was a bright and angry red.

My dad continued with the story. He told me how excited the girl was when she dived into the water, but how difficult she found it to hold her breath. "Chiyo could hold her breath for over a minute, though. And while she was down there, she saw something glinting. She prised it out from between two rocks and shot back up to the surface." He gave a dramatic pause. "It was an abalone shell!"

"What about the girl?" I asked, biting my hand. "Was the girl all right?" I had a feeling that this was going to be a story about how naughty little girls always get their comeuppance, even though I couldn't figure out what I'd done wrong lately to deserve such a tale.

"The girl was fine. Treading water and panting like a dog. Chiyo took her back to the shore, and then she opened up the shell to reveal a large, yellow muscle of meat."

"Yuk," I said through a yawn.

"That's what the girl said too. But people believe that eating abalone keeps you young, and they'll pay top dollar for it. Anyway, this shell was particularly precious, because when Chiyo prodded and poked the creature's gut, she pulled out a pearl."

At this point, my dad stood up, knees clicking, and he started creeping out of the room.

"Daddy?"

"Oh, I thought you'd dropped off."

"Is that the end?"

"That's about the size of it," he said. "Chiyo and the girl went out diving together regularly after that, yadda yadda yadda. The moral of the story is: don't judge a book by the cover. Night, Sol." He shut the door behind him, and I heard his slippers shuffle down the stairs towards the fridge.

I wasn't about to go to sleep, though. The angry red was still blazing inside me. I threw off the covers and watched the fan. I watched the fan for so long that the moving blades began to look like a smooth, spherical object. Like I was looking at a pearl. Or a crystal ball. Or a planet.

8

"Your rockets are pointed in the wrong goddamn direction!" That's what the submarine designer Graham Hawkes once famously shouted at people who believed that space was the final frontier. There's so much left to explore in the depths of our planet's oceans, he said. Why go elsewhere?

When you're on the floor of the North Sea, you can't see much. You might get the occasional beige flicker: a passing cod or pollock. You might even spot a crab scuttling around your feet. But the mud and murk shouldn't deceive you. There's a lot going on down there. And the deeper you go, the better. Once you reach the midnight zone, which is over a thousand metres deep and black as soot—that's where you find the good stuff. For example, the female anglerfish has a lantern growing out of its head. The other fish can't believe their luck when they see the bright light. *Finally*, they think, *there's something in this darkness*. They migrate towards it, mesmerised, and when they get close enough, they're swallowed in a single gulp. I've never been deep enough to see an anglerfish. Almost no human has.

I'm currently in what's known as the Tartan Field. It's a network of wells and pipelines, an underwater industrial estate. Until we've got an alternative sorted, we need places like this. North Sea oil drives our economy. It heats our homes, fuels our cars, paves our roads. It's used in life jackets, tampons, ibuprofen. It's even used to build artificial hearts—it literally keeps hearts beating.

"You ready for this, aye Deano?" asks Hamish, the supervisor on the dive control team. He speaks to me via headphones, and he can see what I'm doing through a camera on my helmet. He's watching Rich too. Today Rich is diver one and I'm diver two. Cal is in the bell. We're working the morning shift, and once we get back to the chamber, the other team will go down.

"Ready as I'll ever be," I say. I've been working for ten hours straight, and I've just finished fixing a pump which feeds oil to a platform over ten miles away. Now I'm retreating while it's powered up to five thousand volts.

"Make sure you don't stand on any connectors as you move back," Hamish says. "Nice and easy."

Walking along the seafloor takes time. It's like wading through treacle, but treacle filled with sharp obstacles which constantly threaten to shred your kit. The most important part, the part that you mustn't break, under any circumstances, is the umbilical. Like a human umbilical, the cord is twisted to prevent tangles. You need to use the cord to find your way back to the bell, but even more critical than that, you need it to keep you alive.

"That's it. Not long until you can go up for your dinner," says Hamish.

It's been a while since I got to witness a pump being tested, and my breath catches in my throat as I wait for it to happen. I imagine the entire North Sea crackling with electricity as I'm fried like a fillet of fish.

Eventually, Hamish speaks. "Nice one, Deano. That's all sorted . . . Deano?"

Looks like I'll live to see another day. I start to retrace my steps. "Yeah?"

"That's all sorted."

"Oh, right, sorry. I'm still here. That's great, Hamish. Cheers for all your help." Normally I'm delighted after a job well done, but today feels like an anticlimax. Something is gnawing at me. It continues to gnaw at me as I enter the diving bell, and it gnaws at me as I take off my helmet, and it gnaws at me as we head back to the saturation chamber, and it gnaws at me as I eat a large portion of lamb stew.

After dinner, I lie on my bunk, and I think about James. He's sent me two text messages, but I've yet to reply. I try not to phone too often, partly because of my helium voice, but also because of the lack of privacy in the chamber. It's not like you can whisper sweet nothings in a place like this.

I'd never used the L-word before I met James. With him, I found it strangely easy. It helped that he had his own life so sorted: his business, his surfing, his board game nights. He didn't need me to complete him; he was complete already. He once told me that I was free to leave whenever I wanted. It was about a year into our relationship. I was getting itchy feet. Not because I wanted to be with anyone else—I just missed my freedom. There's a euphoria that comes with breaking off a relationship. A chance to reinvent yourself, to begin your life anew. I was starting to crave that, and James sensed it.

"I only want to be with you if it's what you want," he told me as we walked home from the pub one night, drunk on an ale called Photon Trails. "If you want to break up with me, I won't put up a fight."

Feeling free to leave made me want to stay. It made me feel free to love.

Two years on, love and freedom don't seem quite so connected. I'm deeply attached to James. I can't imagine what my life would look like without him. So, if I wanted to up sticks one day and head off to, say, Tibet, I'd obviously need to take him into consideration. And if I wanted to go farther afield . . .

Because the truth is, I know what it is that's been gnawing at me.

Mars.

I can't get it out of my head. Even now I'm here, on my dive. It's every adventure I've ever wanted, all wrapped up in one mission. All the training, the physical and psychological preparation. And then, at the end of it all, shooting off the face of Terra Mater, never to return. The idea is so appealing that it makes me want to cry with relief.

"Yo, Deano?" It's Rich. He's peering at me from the bunk above. "You look stoned. Y'all right?"

"Just thinking."

"Ugh, you don't wanna do that. Not while you're in here. 'Scuse my feet." Rich climbs down from his bunk and heads off to the toilet.

While he's gone, I look at the Mars Project website on my phone.

It's not that I'm worried that James would forbid me from entering the competition. For a start, it's so unlikely the mission will happen. But there's a slim possibility it might. And my love for James makes that possibility feel impossible. It's not the green fields or the deep blue sea that I'd miss. It's James.

I scour the competition guidelines yet again. Something that's been playing on my mind is this: to get through to the next round, entrants must write an essay entitled "Why I Want to Be One of the First People to Live on Mars." It sounds like a school project for ten-year-olds. How do you know if someone's cut out to be an astronaut based on some dumb essay? Get them to tackle a military assault course, or put them in a centrifuge, but writing *words*?

Google tells me that the Dutch organisation is funded by a few anonymous private investors—that doesn't exactly fill me with confidence, either. Who's backing this thing? And why does the Mars Project exist in the first place? To take a giant leap across the solar system? Or to put money in pockets that remain firmly on Earth? I can't help but come to the conclusion that the competition is a joke. A scam.

It's a shame, because if I were to enter it, I know I'd be in with a chance. Saturation divers and astronauts are not dissimilar. We're both okay with being locked in confined spaces. We both work in dangerous environments, relying on complex machinery to keep us alive. We both know how it feels to be far away from home. And I'm sure you'd get used to missing people. The brain adjusts, I imagine.

9

"Surface," I say. "I'm ready for the checklist."

"Let's start with communications. Diver helmet? One, two, three, four, five. How do you read me?"

"Five by five."

"Auto-generator? One, two, three, four, five. How do you read me?"

The safety checks go on like this for about half an hour. It's imperative to make sure everything is just so, and although I won't be going into the water today, my role as bellman is essential. I'm responsible for the other two. Any problems, it's down to me to keep us safe. I haven't brought the malachite Anouk gave me into the diving bell, and of course I don't believe in lumps of enchanted rock, but still I find myself making a fist, imagining I'm holding it for a moment.

"Okay, pal," says Hamish on the intercom, once the checks are done. "I'll call the divers in."

"Right, boys," I say, once Cal and Rich have joined me. "Let's get you sorted." I help them put on their gear, making sure they're safe and warm. We all become mothers when it's our turn in the bell. The thought briefly flashes through my mind that I might be pregnant now, and one day the cluster of cells inside me will need me to dress her like this.

It takes about five minutes for the bell to travel through the moon pool and down to the seafloor. That doesn't sound like long, but when there are three of us crammed into this humid metal dome, which is not much bigger than a shower cubicle, it feels like an eternity. Once we've been lowered, I open the hatch and get the guys into the water. They head off in opposite directions, and I set up my hammock. It's much more comfortable than sitting on a stainless steel bench for the next few hours. I keep an eye on the valves and wires and lights ahead of me.

I've been taking the pill for eighteen years. I was roughly halfway through a pack when I stopped. I'm not sure if that means I'm ovulating about now, or if I'll skip that part of my cycle and get an early period. It's bizarre how little I understand about my own anatomy.

I've heard that women feel more aroused around the time they're ovulating. Also, apparently, our faces become more symmetrical and our hip-to-waist ratio becomes more pronounced, making us more attractive to potential mates. Is that happening to me right now? I don't feel aroused or attractive. What if I don't ovulate for a few more days? How long can sperm live inside a woman's reproductive system? Surely James's sperm have either completed their quest or they've croaked. Even if they have fertilised an egg, there's no saying whether the zygote will implant in the lining. Making a baby is a low-chance, high-risk event.

I touch my abdomen through my diving suit. A baby. Trying to imagine it is so abstract that it barely makes sense.

I become aware of Hamish's voice: "Diver two? How's that valve coming on? What's your twenty? Diver two? You copy?"

I check Rich's breathing supply. It looks normal. "Hamish?"

"I can't get a reading on diver two," Hamish tells me. "Give me a minute."

I check Rich's comms and hot water. They look okay too.

"Deano, this is surface," says Hamish. "Prepare for diver rescue."

"Diver rescue. Right. Roger that." I've practised diver rescue multiple times, but I've never had to do it for real.

"Deploy the man lift," Hamish tells me. "Blow the canopy down."

I try to keep calm by imagining this is a drill. I release my standby umbilical, which is two metres longer than Rich's. No matter where he is, I should be able to reach him. If he's stuck, I'll have to try and set him free. We've all heard about the poor guy on Jet Barge 4, who got his arm stuck in a pipe; it sucked the flesh clean off his bones. And we've heard how traumatised the bellman was who found him.

I put on my helmet and lower myself into the water. I take Rich's umbilical in my hand. Even though I know what to do, the moment my body enters the water, I falter.

"Deano? You all set?"

"Big ten-four, Hamish." Despite the hot water being pumped around my suit, I'm shivering. I start to follow the umbilical, taking up slack. I'm observing protocol to the letter, but I don't feel right. I don't know if it's a form of dissociation, which would certainly not be unheard of for me—perhaps it's a way of trying to distract myself from the prospect of coming face-to-face with a co-worker's corpse—but it's hitting me like a ton of bricks: I could be killing my baby right now.

What have I been thinking? Putting my body through all this when there's the possibility of a new life growing inside me? I've known about the risks of diving and pregnancy ever since I started training. Premature delivery, malformed limbs, bubbles in the amniotic fluid. I've read about what happened to rat embryos when they were exposed to hyperbaric oxygen. "Foetal wastage" was the phrase used.

I know about the effects that diving can have on the adult human body too. There are so many things that can go wrong: nitrogen narcosis, barotrauma, pulmonary embolisms, welding accidents, shark attacks, drowning. An American study I once read said that statistically, a commercial diver is forty times more likely to die at work than any other employee. And yet somehow that has never bothered me. Every job has its hazards. I went to school with a girl called Krystal Vickers who got third-degree burns all the way down the left-hand side of her body during a shift at McDonald's. An entire football team got struck by lightning at a match in the Democratic Republic of Congo. An Italian stripper suffocated to death while waiting to jump out of a cake at a stag party. Things happen.

But now I've gone and thrown a baby into the mix. A vulnerable life that I'm responsible for. My baby hasn't consented to the risks I'm exposing myself to. My child shouldn't have to grow up with a hole in her heart because I timed my sex and my work badly. Things happen, yes, but some of them are preventable.

"Deano? You got eyes on diver two?"

It's so muddy down here, I can barely see my own hands. At last, though, I come to the end of the umbilical.

"Um, Hamish," I say faintly. "I've found him."

Rich is reclining, as if on a sun lounger. He looks peaceful. Too peaceful.

"Rich?" I squeeze his shoulder.

His helmet turns. There are air bubbles.

"He's breathing," I say, trying not to let Hamish hear the tremor in my voice. "All right, Rich, it's okay." Talking to Rich is a bit pointless as we don't have a comms line, but it makes me feel better. I open his steady flow valve to give him a bit more air; then I clip my harness onto him.

Rich's body is limp, so I have to carry him back. It's a slow process. Not only is he extremely heavy—even when underwater—but I've also got to be careful not to snag his equipment. Sweating, I hoist Rich into the bell.

"Good work, Solvig," says Hamish, using my name for the first time.

10

"You're a fucking idiot."

It's the first full-blown argument I've witnessed while in saturation. Some of it is hard to make out, as the angrier the guys get, the higher-pitched their voices become. What's clear is that Dale is really laying into Rich.

"What made you think you're cut out for this job?" Dale rants. "In all my years of diving, I've never known such a muppet."

They're at the dining table. Rich obviously wants to leave, but there's nowhere to hide, so he has to sit it out and hope Dale calms down. Eryk is watching TV next to them, but he's put it on silent with the subtitles, out of respect. Every now and then, he looks at Rich, shakes his head, and turns back to *Cash in the Attic*.

Rich leans forwards, cradling his bandaged hand. "If I'd known this would happen, mate . . . but I didn't. I just sort of blacked out. It's only happened a couple of times before. Never on a dive. I thought it was stress."

"Stress?" Dale laughs. "Fucking stress? I'll tell you about stress. Stress is finding out that one of your crew members gets panic attacks from time to time. And that one of those times happens to be while he's wielding heavy fucking machinery. Finding out that he's keeled over and broken his own hand, but it could have been my hand, or . . ." He looks around and points at me. I'm standing stiffly in the doorway. "It could've been her hand. She had to come and chuffing rescue you, you paper hat. Do you know what sort of a situation you put her in?"

"Dale, it's—" I begin.

Surprisingly, it's Eryk who cuts me off, not Dale. "Don't, Deano. We're all getting our pay cut this month because of him. It's ridiculous, man." He looks back at the TV screen, at an old man wearing glasses, running his fingers over a Japanese vase.

I consider picking up where I left off, telling Dale that it's not worth getting into a fight in the chamber, that we should talk about it once we get out, but the thing is, Dale's right. If Rich has been experiencing blackouts, then there's no way he should be allowed to dive. After this, I should think, Rich will be banned from commercial diving for life. Eryk's right about losing our pay too. We haven't even been in the chamber for three full days, and we've already had to start decompressing so Rich can get medical attention.

Losing out on all that money is a nightmare, but what's even worse is having only managed two days of work. I don't have another dive scheduled for seven months. I honestly don't know how I'll handle the wait.

"Look, mate, I'm really sorry," says Rich. "I've been having problems. My wife. She's not handling the dives very well. This is—was—only my fifth dive, but it's already ripping us apart. The fainting episodes only started happening after she—"

"We've all got relationship problems," interrupts Dale. "I've been divorced three times. Eryk's right hand has been his only girlfriend for thirteen years."

Eryk lifts the aforementioned right hand and gives him the middle finger.

"That's diving," Dale continues. "Comes with the territory. You want a happy marriage? Want your kids to love you? Go and get yourself a nice little office job."

Rich slumps over the table, and I can't watch any more. I head for the sleeping chamber. Cal is lying on his bunk with his headphones on, and Tai is nose-deep in his book.

I sit on my bunk. Dale is right. Diving breaks up families. And it's no wonder. Working in conditions like this, being away for weeks at a time.

Suddenly, I realise that I'm crying.

I reach into the back pocket of my rucksack, but instead of feeling the smooth, polished lump of malachite that Anouk gave me, I find fragments.

The stone has shattered.

What was Anouk's warning? *If it turns to dust, watch out.*

I stuff the pieces under my pillow, and I lie in the foetal position. It can't mean anything. It must have had air pockets in it, which exploded at blowdown.

I take my phone out of my pocket and call James. Eight rings before he answers.

"I'm in the middle of a half sleeve," he says. "Okay if I call you back in three hours or so?"

"Three hours," I say. "Sure."

"Is everything all right?" he asks. "Dive going well?"

"Yes," I say, laughing for some reason.

James hangs up, and I put my phone under my pillow next to the chunks of stone. I think I'd put my whole life under a pillow right now if I could.

Tai looks up from his book. "Everything okay, Solvig? You keep sighing."

"Yeah," I say, not very convincingly. "Just taking stock."

Tai's gaze wanders down to my open rucksack, and with a jab of horror I see the prenatal vitamins lying in full view. "Pregnacare," it says in fancy letters on the box.

"So, um, how's your mum?" I blurt, quickly closing my bag.

Tai looks at the floor. "Not good. She's on her second cycle of chemo."

I wish I'd asked him about chopping wood. "I'm really sorry," I say. "I'm here if you ever want to talk."

"Thanks." He focuses on a page of his book.

Tai, I want to say. *I know you've got enough to deal with right now, but . . . help me.*

Instead, Tai speaks. "There is something I'd like to talk about. I'm trying to make a decision."

My heart skips a beat. "I'm trying to make a decision too."

"Should I do a course on French cabinetmaking?" Tai asks. "Or learn to build string instruments?"

"Oh," I say. "Instruments?"

"Specifically, learning how to craft lutes."

I frown, then surprise myself with a laugh. "Nobody plays the lute any more."

Tai snorts. "Sting plays the lute."

"*Sting*? Okay. You've convinced me. Go with the lutes."

"I think you're right," Tai replies. "So . . . what was yours, then? The thing you're trying to decide about?"

I look over at Cal. He's facing the wall, still wearing headphones. It's how he deals with stress: to check out. In fact, it's how he deals with dives in general. He's a good bloke, but nobody really knows him. I once asked him what kind of music he was into and he said novelty ragtime.

I look back at Tai and prop myself up on my elbows. "There's this thing I'm doing at the moment. But there's this other thing I want to do. It's not easy to do both things at once."

"Is it something to do with those tablets?"

My cheeks burn. "That's not the thing I'm thinking about giving up."

"What is it, then?"

"Do you ever feel selfish?" I ask. "For doing what we do?"

"Everything is selfish," Tai says. "Diving is selfish. Having children is selfish. You can feel guilty about anything if you try hard enough."

"Is making lutes selfish?"

Tai laughs. "Most definitely." He turns back to his book.

I send James a text to say I'll talk to him tomorrow; then I put my phone away. The light in the chamber is so bright that it takes me a long time to get to sleep.

11

What time is it? I grope for my phone, but it's not there. This isn't my bunk. I remember now.

After an awkward five-and-a-half-day wait, we got out of the saturation chamber. The cold winds of the North Sea slapped me in the face, but they were welcome.

I decided not to go home. I rented a car and drove out to the Cairngorms. The original plan was to find a room with a view, but, tired as I was, I couldn't bring myself to stop the car. I drove all the way to the west coast, adding an extra five hours onto my journey. It's hard to pinpoint exactly why I did that. I used to live on this side of the country, and I did my dive training here, so perhaps I was feeling sentimental.

I've ended up renting a shepherd's hut in Kilchoan. If I don't get to live in a saturation chamber for the next three weeks, then this narrow space will do. It's freezing, though. How long have I been asleep?

I haul my feet over the side of the bed. My phone is on a table near the bed. I squint at the screen. It's 4:30 a.m. on

Saturday, which means I've been asleep for nearly two days. God. The decompression always knocks me out, but this is a new record.

Thankfully, there's a socket in here so my phone is fully charged. "Solar power," the woman who owns the hut boasted as she showed me around. I didn't tell her I work in the oil industry.

I use the light of my phone to check out the wood-burning stove. Took me ages to get this going when I first arrived, so I hope I can manage it now. I screw up a few sheets of newspaper from the basket next to the stove. My fingers are so cold they're not working properly. I open the stove, throw in the paper, and sprinkle on a handful of kindling. After two failed attempts, I light a match.

"Please," I say under my breath, as I close the stove door.

Next, I light tea lights in a couple of lanterns, pleased I haven't had to use the electric lamp. The candlelight makes me feel as though I'm in some in-between place, where it's neither night nor day.

I take a look around the hut. It's got wood panelling on the walls, an embroidered quilt on the bed, and mismatching furniture. I like it. The woman who runs the place, Lizzie, lives in a farmhouse up the hill. She told me she'd left a few bits and bobs to get me started. There's a tin of beans, some bread rolls, and a bowl of eggs. I take an egg and press my fingertip against a small white feather stuck to the shell. I put it back in the bowl.

I get the beans going on the gas hob, noting happily that even in a place like this, there is a need for the oil industry. I sit on the wicker chair.

Well. Here I am.

I found the hut online. When I knocked on the farmhouse door, it was nine in the morning. I could see into the kitchen: a man and woman were sitting on wooden rocking chairs in front of a bottle-green range. Two girls were playing with a toy train at their feet. The man was smoking a pipe, and the woman was reading the paper. Something about that Dickensian scene made such sense to me. Fate had brought me out of the water and all the way to this farmhouse. I could have been on the seabed at that moment, turning screws and melting metal, but instead, here I was, peering at a family tableau.

The woman, Lizzie, patted the girls' heads before she came to answer the door. "How long will you be staying, dearie?" she asked.

As long as it takes, I felt like answering. I told her I'd start with three nights and take it from there.

"You're here during our quiet period," she told me. "No one's booked in for a wee while, so just let me know what's good for you."

What's good for me. How do I figure that one out?

I stir the beans and think about babies. I think about diving and my dad and long-distance running and looking at the stars and vodka and my dog. It's like that four burners theory everyone was going on about a few years ago. Your life is a cooker with four burners—or hobs or rings or whatever you want to call them—representing work, health, friends, and family. The theory is that if you want to be successful, you have to turn off at least one burner. If you want to be extremely successful, you have to turn off two. How many burners does it take to make a baby? It takes one to make beans.

I take the saucepan off the stove and pour the contents over a bread roll. I balance the plate on my knees and eat. This meal reminds me of a camping trip James and I went on when we first got together. Our Trangia broke on the first night (so, no burners at all), and we had to eat sachets of mushroom stroganoff and freeze-dried Moroccan chicken prepared with cold water. We were hiking around the Lake District at the time, and I was determined to finish the trip without having to stop off at Millets for supplies. James argued that going to Millets wasn't cheating, but it felt like it to me.

That trip was one of our first dates. We'd met only a fortnight or so earlier, in a snooker hall in Huddersfield. I'd been at a friend's thirtieth, getting pampered at a spa hotel. Not my thing. At the end of it, full of lavender and soapsuds, I was desperate to go somewhere grimy again. I happened upon this snooker hall and thought, *Why not?* It reminded me of the many hours I'd spent at the Eastville Social Club with my dad when I was a girl.

James was there on a stag do, and he had escaped to the bar while his mates were finishing a game. That's where we got talking. Before long, we were flirting so much that we'd swapped numbers, French-kissed, and arranged a week-long hiking trip to the Lake District. It was out of character for me, but then so was James. I think I always went for jerks in the past because I knew they wouldn't last. James's good nature was exciting and scary in equal measure.

I didn't know when we spoke that first time that James had been in a car accident and had his lower left leg amputated. When he mentioned it on the phone a few days later, it was only because he wanted to reassure me that it wouldn't get in the way of our camping trip. We met up at my place in Liverpool the following day. James drove for eight hours to visit me. I couldn't wait to rip off all his clothes and see what lay beneath the surface. That prosthetic leg made James seem even more edgy. I say "even more" because he also had long hair, tattoos, and a pierced cheek. He wasn't just a nice guy; he was an exotic species.

We didn't have sex that night, as it happens. We baked a beef Wellington.

I finish my beans and put my empty plate on the side, ready to wash under the outside tap in the morning. I put a log on the fire and climb back into bed. I could do a bit of reading. I finished the folktales during decompression, but I've still got the thriller James gave me. *Little Deaths.*

That reminds me of something. I look at my phone and search for information on congenital disorders among children of divers.

My period still hasn't come since I stopped taking the pill. I really need to stop wondering if I'm pregnant, though. People try to conceive for years. It's so unlikely that it will have worked first time. And if it has worked . . .

I reach for the wooden hatch above me and slide it back to reveal a Velux window. I can see the night sky, speckled with stars: the Milky Way. Or the Milky *Circle*, which was apparently the ancient Greek name for our galaxy. They believed that stars were the goddess Hera's breast milk, splashed across the sky. I like the Greek name better than ours, because calling it a circle reminds me that it's always there, wrapped around us like a motherly hug.

12

"Another Oban, please."

"Right you are," says the woman behind the bar.

I'm at the Kilchoan Hotel, working my way through a bottle of fourteen-year-old single malt. Tastes of cigarettes and disinfectant. I'm avoiding contact with James so that I don't have to tell him I'm out of saturation. At least I feel connected to him by having his favourite drink.

I should probably eat. I've had all my meals in the hut so far, throwing together whatever I can get from the local shop. Spaghetti hoops, Dolmio pasta pouches, Super Noodles. The Ardnamurchan beefburger should be exactly what I fancy, but even though I've had an active day, I'm not hungry.

This morning I climbed to the summit of Ben Hiant. Lizzie told me it's a "must" if I'm going to be staying all week. She even lent me some crampons. On a clear day, at the top of the hill, you can get panoramic views across islands that sound like settings for fairy tales: Tiree, Coll, Rum, Eigg. This morning started off clear, but by the time I got to the summit, I could see only the ground beneath my feet.

After that, I went back to the hut and started the crime novel, which is based on a true story: two children are murdered in New York in the sixties, and the prime suspect is the mother. She's a good-looking divorcee who drinks, smokes, and wears lipstick, so clearly she's not to be trusted. Twenty pages in, I decided to walk to the nearest pub.

The barmaid hands me a whisky, and I add a splash of water from a pottery jug that says "Teacher's" on it. Then I sit in an armchair by the open fire and close my eyes.

"Mind if I join you, hen?"

I look up and see a man, maybe sixty, dressed in faded jeans and a checked shirt. He's got a bushy grey beard and has a definite lumberjack look about him.

"No, no, please do." I shift back, as if making room for him on my chair.

He takes the chair opposite and lets out a long, artificial sigh. "That's better. It's Baltic out there. Plays havoc with the chilblains." He puts his beer on the table. The label says "Vital Spark." He holds his hands up to the fire. "You looked a million miles away then, lass."

I have a mouthful of whisky and wonder if it'd be rude to close my eyes again. "I wish I was a million miles away," I say.

The man laughs. "Ach, you're always a million miles away from somewhere." He takes a long draught from his bottle. Indulges in another artificial sigh. "Good stuff, this," he says. "Brewed in Fort William. Slightly less than a million miles away." He chuckles, as do I. "What brings you to Kilchoan? I'm presuming you're no local. The accent. The hiking gear. The look of someone who's come here to get away and is no really wanting an auld fool blethering on at her when she's come in for a bit of peace and quiet."

"I'm actually supposed to be working right now," I say. Revealing this makes me feel lighter, like a secret has been unloaded. I continue: "I'm a diver in the North Sea, but my dive was cut short, so I drove here from Aberdeen instead of going home." There: that is my confession. Maybe, somehow, via the movement of particles or energy, James has been able to absorb that admission from his position in Cornwall.

"A diver, eh?" The man scratches his beard. "We had a diver die out here last October. In the Sound of Mull. The RNLI took him to hospital, but he didn't make it. Terrible business."

The last thing I need is yet another person telling me what a dangerous career I'm in. The greatest danger divers face is being told how dangerous their job is every five minutes. So I ask: "What do you do for a living?"

"I work up at the Lighthouse."

"You're a lighthouse keeper?"

He throws back his head and howls with laughter. "I work in the coffee shop. Keeping myself busy. Weans are at uni, you see. I'm what's known as an empty nester."

"I'm trying for a baby," I tell him. It's a sudden, knee-jerk response to the mention of children. Another admission. Another lightened load.

"Oh, aye," he replies. "It can be, it can be. How long have you been trying for, if you don't mind me asking?"

I purse my lips. "Technically, one day."

The man doesn't laugh, as I expect him to, but nods slowly. "Well, good luck, hen. I hope it works out for you."

I feel stupid now. The whisky is like truth serum. "I'd better get back," I say, forcing out a yawn.

"You're not staying at the hotel?"

"No, it's just a short walk away." I notice that I'm being protective about where exactly I'm headed. I think I trust this man. But I don't trust men.

"Right you are." He winks. "Mind out for wild beasties on your way home."

I button my parka all the way to my chin. There are no street lamps outside, and I don't have a flashlight, so I take out my phone and shine its pathetic greenish light ahead of me.

Ten minutes later, I hear a scream. It's coming from one of the fields. It's a woman.

I stop, rigid, listening.

There it is again. The first time I heard it, I thought it was a scream of pain. This time it sounds different. It's a war cry.

•

I can barely breathe when Lizzie answers the door.

"I'm an idiot," I say, panting. "Can you help me?"

"Och, you look freezing," Lizzie says. "Do you want to come in?"

I put my hand to my mouth. "I just left a woman for dead."

Lizzie takes her coat from a hook by the door. "A woman? Where?"

"Up towards the hotel. I heard a scream. Two screams. Coming from the fields."

Lizzie pauses, arm midway through her coat sleeve. "Did it sound like this?" She imitates the scream.

"You heard it too?"

Lizzie laughs. "That'll be a wildcat, dearie. It's mating season."

"Oh," I say. "I was right about being an idiot."

Lizzie squeezes my shoulder. "You're not the first to make that mistake. Now listen, did you have a good time earlier? Up Ben Hiant?"

I'm still panting. I hope my breath doesn't stink of whisky. "Yes. Thanks for the crampons." I put my palms together in a prayer position. "I think I'm going to head home in the morning."

"Nae bother," Lizzie says, unaware of the momentousness of the decision I've just made.

As she advises me about checkout, I hear her daughters squawking like parrots in the kitchen. Before I turn to leave, I consider, for a split second, whether it would be appropriate to ask Lizzie to meet them. Obviously, the answer is no. Not my family. Not appropriate.

Back at the hut, I get the fire going and pace up and down. Two steps in one direction, two in the other. This tiny space doesn't feel as reassuring as it did before.

I light all the candles in the hut, switch on the electric light by the bed, and send James a text. *Back tomorrow*, I tell him. *Dive cut short.*

Now, I set about cooking up every item of food I have left in the hut. My blood is pumping, my slate is clear, my appetite is back.

That four burners theory is a load of rubbish.

I'm going to switch on all my burners, all at once, and see what happens.

13

Entrant: Solvig Dean

Title: Why I Want to Be One of the First People to Live on Mars

Ever since I was a little girl, I've wanted to do something so momentous that it alters the course of humankind forever.

Does that sound narcissistic? Maybe it is. I'm just not satisfied with small achievements. A job promotion here, a marathon there. Nice as those things are, they don't help propel humanity into a new era.

When I was five, I watched a programme about the Apollo 11 space mission. I learnt about how Armstrong and Aldrin almost crashed into the moon, only surviving by the skin of their teeth. I remember my dad saying something like: "Ruddy hell, kid, who'd put themselves through something like that?" And I remember looking up at him, smiling sweetly, and saying: "Me, Daddy. I would." My dad probably laughed, ruffled my hair, and asked if I wanted a chocolate Nesquik.

Now that I'm older, I'm wiser. I know what happened on the first Apollo mission. When Grissom and the others couldn't evacuate the spacecraft during a fire, and they burned to death before they'd even set off.

And I know what happened to the cosmonauts in *Soyuz 11* as they were returning from the Soviet space station. How they looked after their spacecraft landed, strapped to their seats, blood oozing from their ears.

And I know what happened to Christa McAuliffe, the teacher who beat ten thousand applicants in a competition to be the first private citizen to be sent to space. I've seen footage of the kids on the ground, eagerly counting her down to lift-off, and I've seen the horror on their faces two minutes later.

I know what Ronald Reagan said when he addressed the nation afterwards too. "It's hard to understand, but sometimes painful things like this happen." His white handkerchief was poking out of his jacket pocket as he looked straight into the camera. "It's all part of the process of exploration and discovery," he said, unwavering. "It's all part of taking a chance and expanding man's horizons. The future doesn't belong to the faint-hearted."

When I think about those words, they make me want to shout out affirmations to the universe.

I want to expand man's horizons!

I want to take a chance!

Pain is part of the process!

PART TWO

14

"The thing I love most about Caribbean food," says James, "is that it's such an interesting fusion of cuisines." He washes down his curried goat with a mouthful of Jamaican Ting. "African, Cajun, Indonesian," he continues. "Creole, Asian, European. I mean, there are so many influences."

I'm having ackee and saltfish with rice and plantain. "Yeah," I say, reaching for my mocktail. "It's tasty."

It's our three-year anniversary today. Three years since we first had sex, in a tent in the Lake District. I broach this. "Do you remember that first night in the Lakes? Where was it we were staying? Somewhere near Buttermere?"

"Wasdale Head," says James. "By Scafell Pike. There was that woman who had a tick on her back. You had to pull it out with tweezers."

I smile. "Yes. And then she gave us those scones as a thank-you. We couldn't eat them because the raisins looked like ticks."

James grimaces. "I love you."

"Love you too," I echo.

After the Lakes, I left my place in Liverpool and followed James down to Falmouth. As a way of forcing myself to stay in one place for a while, I decided to buy somewhere. The plan wasn't necessarily for James to move in with me, but he did. Not stopping to think it through is probably what made it work. We just got on with it.

"A big reason that the Caribbean is a melting pot of so many different cultures," says James, skewering another lump of meat, "is down to its bloody past."

One of the waiters is looking at us.

"This saltfish is delicious," I say. "Want to try some?"

James leans towards me, and I guide the fork into his open mouth. *Here comes the aeroplane . . .*

I'm expecting James to give me a detailed flavour profile of the mouthful he's eaten, but instead he says: "Listen, Solvig. I'm finding trying for a baby with you to be really gratifying. But if you ever feel like you're not ready, then say."

"I want to do it. I do. Honestly." I raise my mocktail and we clink glasses.

The shepherd's hut happened three months ago. I told James everything when I got back. About Rich. About leaving saturation early. About driving to the west coast to get my head straight.

Well, I guess I didn't tell James everything. I didn't mention applying for the Mars Project. But why bother him with that? It'd be like stirring a pot that doesn't need stirring.

Since returning to Falmouth, I've tried to get on with normal life. I've been running every day. I've eaten loaf after loaf of sourdough. I've had coffee with Anouk a couple of times while Nike's at school. Anouk still looks tired, but she hasn't doled out any more magic stones—and I haven't told her what happened to the last one. Haven't told her about trying for a baby either. Apart from that, it's business as usual.

My periods are back. An article in the paper recently said that over 60 percent of people trying for a baby conceive after three months. Over 80 percent conceive within a year. My next dive is in August.

The newspaper article also said that after deciding to try for a baby, couples have sex an average of seventy-eight times before getting pregnant. Since I returned from Scotland, we haven't had sex anywhere close to that number of times. But we did decide to quit drinking four weeks ago, after reading that it helps. Other things I'm doing: drinking decaf coffee, using an ovulation tracker app, and thinking maternal thoughts. Like, for instance, when I see a baby, I think about how nice it might feel to kiss its head or rub ointment onto its bottom.

But the article said other things too. Bad things. About how a woman's fertility deteriorates exponentially as she gets closer to forty. Not just affecting her chances of conceiving in the first place, but affecting everything: pregnancy complications, birth defects. If a woman has her first baby when she's over thirty-five, the article said, she's deemed a "geriatric mother." I turned thirty-seven in February.

"What do you fancy doing after this?" James asks. "We could go to the cinema. There's that film *Rampage*, about a silverback gorilla who genetically mutates into a monster."

I shake my head. "Let's just go home and have sex."

A young couple walks into the restaurant. Probably students. The girl's lips are a wild shade of pink, and she exudes a confidence belied only by the magenta lines on the back of her hand: a tally of lipstick testers counting off the hours to go before her date.

"Would you like it if I wore make-up?" I ask James.

"I'd like you to do whatever you like," he responds.

"But would it turn you on?"

He puts his hand on mine. "Seeing you happy turns me on. Speaking of which, I got you something. For our anniversary."

We don't normally bother with anniversary gifts. I haven't even bought James a card.

"I know we've said we aren't going on holiday this year," James says. "You know, in case the timing is wrong."

I don't remember agreeing to that. My hand drops first to my abdomen, then my thighs.

"So instead of a holiday," James continues, "I've used the money I've been putting aside for something else." He reaches into his trouser pocket and pulls out a small black cube.

I hope that's not what I think it is. If it is, the answer's no.

"Here we go." He opens up the tiny box. Inside is a silver ring studded with a line of diamonds. "It's not an engagement ring. Don't worry. I know how you feel about marriage. It's an eternity ring."

"An eternity ring?"

"To symbolise our never-ending love," James explains. "Technically, this is a half-eternity ring, because I couldn't afford stones all the way around." He takes it out of the box. "But the symbolism is the same."

I can't hide my shock. For my birthday, James got me an os-cillating hoe and an ergonomic garden trowel. This is no trowel.

"I don't know what to say," I stutter. Do I need to be on my guard every time we come out for food from now on? When James asked if I wanted to try for a baby, we were in a café. Now, it's an eternity ring in a Caribbean restaurant. What next? Getting engaged in a chophouse? Renewing our vows at an all-you-can-eat buffet?

"You don't have to say anything," James tells me. "Wear it and enjoy."

Hesitantly, I push the band onto my left-hand ring finger. The marriage finger. It looks like a mistake. Something so deli-cate, so sparkly, on me. "Thank you. I didn't get you anything. I feel overwhelmed. I'm sorry."

"It suits you," James says, with a look of pride. I'm not sure if he's talking about the ring, or the notion of being with him for eternity.

15

"Can I play with Mr. Wobble now, Soffig?"

Finally, Anouk has taken me up on my offer of babysitting. I got a call from her late last night.

"It's time I made some space for myself again," she said breathlessly. "So I'm trying out a new yoga class."

It's the first time Anouk has asked anyone to look after Nike. This evening, after she put her coat on, it took her twenty minutes to leave the house. She hovered in the hallway, checking and rechecking that I had everything I needed.

"Just go," I laughed, practically pushing her out of the door.

Anouk stood on the doorstep. "You'll be okay, won't you? Make sure he has his cocoa before bed."

It might have been nerves, but I swear Anouk seemed shifty. She wasn't looking me in the eye. I wonder if the yoga is a smokescreen. She could be on a date. That would be the first time she's gone out with anyone since I've known her. I didn't even realise that she was a lesbian when we first became friends. It didn't come up in conversation for months—not because Anouk was trying to hide it. She's just happy being single. And she was insistent about wanting to adopt a child without anyone else in the picture. "Why complicate things further?" she once told me with a shrug. But having a kid has brought out a new, softer side to her. So, who knows?

We haven't had one of our red-wine-fuelled heart-to-hearts for ages. I remember one such evening at the Star & Garter, on "Bluegrass and Brisket" night. As always, the place was buzzing, and it gave me a strange boldness with my best friend.

"I nearly kissed a woman once," I told her.

"You'd better not be coming on to me, Solvig Dean." Anouk waggled a finger at me, eyes sparkling, lips plump and wine-stained.

"Wouldn't dream of it." I winked. I'm not sure why I was flirting. I didn't see Anouk as anything other than a friend. I never have. I mean, she's gutsy, clever, gorgeous. Her parents are Buddhist volleyball players: she's of the coolest stock. But I'm straight and she's my boyfriend's friend. Boring, but true.

"So," Anouk said, leaning across the table, raising her voice above the bluegrass, "why didn't you kiss her?"

"It was when I was doing my dive training. She had a shaved head and looked so tough I didn't dare speak to her for, like, the first five classes."

"That's so you," said Anouk.

"But on the last day, she stopped me as I was heading out of the building. She practically pinned me against the wall. Told me she'd got herself a job in the Gulf of Mexico—God knows how. Said she was leaving in a week. Asked if I wanted to go for a drink."

"And you were tempted?"

"I said no to the drink, but I very nearly leaned in for a kiss. She was attractive—like Demi Moore in *G.I. Jane*. But you know what did it for me? She was about to leave the country. That's what appealed."

Anouk laughed. "I don't think that's all it was."

I thought I understood what Anouk meant when she said that at the time, but now I wish I'd asked her to explain.

"Soffig? Can I play with Mr. Wobble?"

Nike is sitting cross-legged on the carpet, looking up at me with big, dark eyes.

"Sorry, sweetie. I was daydreaming. I'll get your toy out of the cupboard and you can play with it while I make you some cocoa. How about that?"

Nike nods.

I get up off the sofa and fetch Mr. Wobble. I've seen Nike playing with this thing before. It's a wooden clown shaped like an egg, with a weight in the base, so that even when you push it over, it rights itself.

"Take that, Wobble-Gobble!" shouts Nike, as he punches Mr. Wobble in the abdomen.

I head into the kitchen feeling proud of myself. I'm not bad at this parenting business.

Anouk's left a tin of cocoa on the counter. I shake some into a saucepan of milk and put the pan on the hob. I'm not sure what to do next. Do you add sugar? I chuck in a couple of spoonfuls to be sure.

I can't help noticing my eternity ring as I pour the mixture out into a mug. My hand looks like it belongs to someone else.

"Come on then, big boy." I head into the living room, where Nike is flicking his toy clown in the face. "Time for your cocoa." I sit and pat the sofa beside me.

Nike's jaw drops. "We don't have cocoa in here, stupid. We take it upstairs to my bedroom and then you tell me a bedtime story. That's what Mummy does." This is the first time I've heard Nike refer to Anouk as his mum. I'm so taken aback by it that it takes me a moment to respond.

"Okay, chicken. Let's go up. Leave Mr. Wobble on the carpet. I'll put him away for you. That's it. Chop-chop." Where are all these words coming from? *Big boy? Chicken? Chop-chop?*

He gets down on all fours and begins climbing the stairs slowly and clumsily.

"Is that how Mummy likes you to go upstairs?" I ask dubiously.

"Uh-huh," he pants theatrically.

When we reach the top, Nike takes me into his room.

"What about your teeth?"

"Mum lets me do them in the morning."

This doesn't sound plausible. I'll get him to brush them after the story. For now, I tell him to put on his pyjamas while I select a book from his shelf.

"Don't read one of them," he says, racing over to his chest of drawers and pulling out a pair of striped pyjamas. "I've heard them a million times. Make something up."

"I don't know if I can do that," I laugh, trying to disguise my fear. I've never made up a story before. I don't know how it works. Do you know what the ending will be before you begin? Do you make it up sentence by sentence? Do you start with a character? Or a setting?

I look up at the ceiling as Nike starts changing. He has the same glow-in-the-dark stars that I had as a kid. His walls are painted blue, and there's a wallpaper border featuring cartoon rockets and planets. "Are you into space, Nike?"

"What do you mean?" His tone of voice suggests that he's struggling with something. I look over and see his head is stuck inside his pyjama top, and he's naked on the bottom half. Is it appropriate for me to help him get dressed? Fortunately, as I'm wavering, he pulls his head through the correct hole and follows my gaze, which has now moved back to the wall.

"Oh yes, *that* space," he says. "I like space. I like trucks and stegosauruses and questions too."

"Questions?"

"Yes." He begins putting on his pyjama bottoms. "I've got a question for you. How big is a stegosaurus's brain?"

I perch on the end of his bed. "This big?" I ask, stretching my arms wide apart, doing the old grown-up trick of pretending I think something is much bigger than it really is. My outstretched arms almost touch the walls on each side of his room. It's not much smaller in here than a saturation chamber, which would sleep six adults.

"Dummy. It's the size of a Ping-Pong ball!" Nike leaps onto the bed, giggling. I hope he's not getting hyper.

"Come on, pup," I say. "Under the covers." I prop him up with pillows and hand him his mug.

Nike scrapes the wrinkled skin off the top of the cocoa with his finger. "I like eating the skin," he says, sucking his fingertip, and then downing his entire drink in two goes. He grins and shows me his teeth, a brown scummy film smeared across them.

"Okay, mister," I say. "Story time." I think back to the stories my dad used to tell me. They seem so complicated when I try and remember them now. I'm going to have to invent something from scratch.

"This is a story about an astronaut," I begin. "An astronaut who decides to live in outer space."

Nike wriggles under the covers and looks up at me expectantly.

"The astronaut—who is called Rik—doesn't have a wife or children. He's always been too consumed by his work to have time for that sort of thing. One day, Rik tells NASA that he wants to go and live on the moon. He says that he might even like to start a colony there. Of course, NASA is very excited by the proposition. They tell Rik that he deserves to have dreams as big as this one. What's more, they have the power to make his dreams come true."

The rocket hasn't even left the launchpad yet, but Nike begins to snore. I slowly count down from ten to zero.

16

"So good of you to pop up and see your old man," says my dad, for the hundredth time since I arrived. He turns to his carer. "Reveka, show Sol that thing you showed me last night."

Reveka gives my father a definite look. "It's really not so great," she says. "Just something my kid showed me." Reveka has hunched shoulders, and a mouth that's reluctant to smile. She's probably very good for my father.

My dad is a scoundrel and a womaniser. If his boasts are true, then roughly three-quarters of his carers have ended up in bed with him. Never refers to them as girlfriends, though. It's easier to end a business relationship.

"Go on," my dad urges.

"Whatever it is, I'd love to see it," I say politely, wondering how much longer we all have to sit around the kitchen table before I get a cuppa. I know I should offer to make one myself, but even though I grew up in this house, I feel as if I'm a guest these days.

It's comforting to be here, in any case. This 1930s semi-detached home still has the same kitchen cabinets that my mother installed. Her magnolia brushstrokes still adorn some of the walls. And although the house is close to a part of Bristol that has recently become a hipster haven, it's thankfully positioned a good forty-minute walk away from the micropubs and coffee roasters. Here, the houses still flaunt grey pebble-dash and uPVC front doors. They're not decorated in the bright colours that Bristol is famous for. I'm not ready for my childhood to be hidden behind those colours just yet.

"It's a trick," my dad tells me, and I realise I've been staring into space. "With fridge magnets. Go and fetch 'em, Reveka." It's good to see him happy. Takes years off him. Even though he's still got all his own hair—a thick and lustrous brown—there was a period of time last year when I began to refer to him as "elderly." I'm sure he was depressed, though he never admitted it. And I never built up the courage to ask him.

Reveka sighs as she goes over to the fridge. She peels two flat magnets off the door and comes back to the table.

My dad elbows me. "Wait till you see this. Hurry up, Reveka, doll."

It's hard to get an idea of my dad's good side if you spend only ten minutes in his company. Last night, though, while I was babysitting Nike, it hit me: my dad did a good job bringing me up. He protected me from the grief that crouched in the corners of our house. And he told stories that made me feel like I had the power to achieve great things.

I was so keen to speak to him last night that I barely even stopped to hear Anouk tell me how her class had gone.

"Lots of stretching," she told me. "Very relaxing."

I got out my phone before I'd even left the house. The first thing I said when my dad answered was: "I miss you." I don't think I've ever told him that before.

"Okay, so here's a couple of magnets," says Reveka. "As you can see, they're just ordinary fridge magnets."

I humour her and take a good look. One has a picture of Prague on it. The other says "Fuck fibromyalgia."

Reveka turns them over, then places the shiny black sides together. "If you go like this, they move up and down really easily." She slides them against each other in a vertical motion. "But if you go the other way, like this"—she slides them back and forth horizontally—"they get a bit stuck. Try it."

I take the magnets and rub them against one another as Reveka did. They keep catching, making a small clicking noise.

"Eh?" says my dad. "How about that?"

Reveka takes the magnets back to the fridge and reattaches them. "Fuck fibromyalgia" is upside down. "It's not really a trick," she says. "It's just the way fridge magnets are made."

"Because of where the poles are," says my dad, eyeing up Reveka's behind. "They make 'em in strips. Good, innit?"

My reaction is a noise somewhere between "mmm" and "oh." "Moh."

"She's good with tricks, is Reveka." Dad gives Reveka a wink, and she rolls her eyes.

I scrape back my chair. "Tea, anyone?"

Reveka's expression changes from amusement to horror. "Oh no, I forgot. I'll make the drinks. Why don't you two go and sit in the living room?"

My dad stands with a groan, and I help him out into the hall. As soon as we're clear of the doorway, he gives me a conspiratorial smile. "Come this way," he whispers, opening the door to the garage. "Don't tell Reveka I brought you in here, eh?"

I shrug. "All right."

My dad has had to give up welding as a career, but the garage still looks like a haven of industry. In the centre of the room, a coatrack with hooks made of horseshoes is in mid-construction.

"She encourages me to do it," he says, gesturing towards the kitchen. "But she doesn't like me coming in here when it's cold. Given me a new lease of life though, it has, getting back into it." He runs his fingers along one of the horseshoes on the coatrack. "Gets everywhere, this rust."

As well as suffering from fibromyalgia and having undergone spine fusion surgery, my dad's also blind in one eye. The year before I was born, he was cutting a pipe and some slag flew in. You'd think he'd have learnt his lesson and worn goggles after that, but I recall him suffering from arc eye—sunburn of the retina—several times while I was growing up. He had to use artificial tears, which always struck me as ironic, because he used to cry so many real ones.

Dad picks up a pink manila folder off his worktop and waves it in the air. "Anyway, this is why I've brought you in here. I was having a clear-out the other day and found this old thing in the filing cabinet. Some stuff I kept from your mum's desk. Maybe you'd like to keep it? Sentimental value or whatever."

I take the folder. "Really? This was Mum's? You don't mind me keeping it?"

Dad's mouth contorts into a strange upside-down grin. "Nah. I won't be around forever. You have it, kiddo. Probably total crap anyway." I wonder why he always has to do that: catastrophise, hyperbolise. Keepsakes are crap. Disappointments are disasters. He's never ill, he's utterly fucked.

"Thanks, Dad." I press the folder to my chest. "I'd love to have it."

"We'll go and sit in the warm now, eh?" We trudge back into the house.

Reveka is perched on one end of the sofa with three mugs lined up on the coffee table. She tuts. "You've been in the garage."

"You know, Rev, babe," my dad says, "I think I'll go and lie down for a bit." He gives a melodramatic yawn.

"Oh, right. Sure." Reveka springs up out of her seat.

"Reveka's tucking me in, pup," he explains, in an unfamiliar, childlike voice. "We'll be out later on, in time for dinner. You'll be all right, won't you?"

Before I have the chance to answer, he and Reveka are gone, leaving me with three undrunk cups of tea. I try to push the thought that maybe they've gone to have sex out of my mind.

I take my drink upstairs, stopping briefly in the hallway to look at the old oak bookcase. Dad's had this thing since before I was born. Barely a scratch on it. The books on the shelves aren't in such good condition, though. Almost all of them were Mum's. Organised alphabetically: Asimov, Bradbury, Clarke. Dad told me that Mum used to read them in the bath. As a girl, I would run my fingertips over the pages. Warped by the steam of my mother's bathwater, they rippled like waves on the sea. Now that I'm older, I've thought about borrowing a couple of them—taking them to read while in saturation, perhaps—but I can't bring myself to do it. I like them here, on the shelves. Dad's shrine to Mum.

I go into my room, which I still call *my* room, even though it's used for the carers now—well, for the ones that don't stay in Dad's room with him, at any rate. I can't remember which carer it was that redecorated, but it's the only room in the house that's completely changed since I lived here. Gone is the toothpaste-green paint I chose for the walls. The Dr. Pepper stain on the carpet in the corner. The Jacques Cousteau poster hanging over the radiator, and the NASA sticker on the skirting board. Now the walls are blue, with curtains and carpet to match.

I sit on the bed (new mattress) and take a few mouthfuls of tea. It's very weak. Not worth the wait.

I put down the mug, then run my fingers over the folder in my lap. I wonder whether my mum bought it. Whether it came in a multicoloured pack, or if she chose pink specifically. Whether she always went for the manila folder style, or if she used ring binders. Most of all, I wonder what I'll find inside. I almost don't want to open it, though. It's like unwrapping a present at Christmas. The anticipation is the best bit.

I take out the first sheet of paper, marvelling at the fact that it's at least thirty-four years old. How long does it take for paper to disintegrate? Should I be wearing white gloves? I hold the paper lightly between finger and thumb. It's perforated down each side, with holes punched into the margins. I'd forgotten about this—what was it called? Something futuristic. Matrix paper?

The words printed on the page are in a grey Courier New font. They are technical and wise. I don't understand them at all.

I pull out the next page and immediately feel as though I've hit the jackpot. It's got *handwriting* on it. The writing is similar to mine, but a little softer, rounder. There are phrases scrawled in different directions across the page, all in blue ballpoint: "IBM compatible," "replacing the complex commands of the operating system with plain English," and "a simple 'point and click' technique." Around the phrases are doodles. No pictures, just shapes. In one corner, there's a tight honeycomb of hexagons, and in another, my mother has encased a small square inside several larger ones. What can I learn about her from these doodles? She liked shapes. A lot of people doodle faces or animals or the name of the person they love. Not my mum. Her doodles look like the inside of a computer.

Next, I pull out a sheet of A4 paper. There's handwriting on this one too. It's spidery and off-kilter—written while drunk, maybe? Or did it erupt out in a moment of intellectual fervour? It looks like a flow chart. There are mysterious labels inside the boxes: "Dense Forest," "Drive Bubble Entrance," "Red Hall," "Nesting Cage," and "Melted Spot." The lines between the boxes are labelled with letters: *P, S, A, F, U,* and *D*. Around the edge of the paper, my mum has written cryptic notes: "Put red rod in second red slot in repair room to fix air?" Looks like she was designing her own computer game. Maybe she was designing something for *me* to play? Here's an example of her genius, in black ballpoint. I feel light-headed.

As I reach into the folder to see what's next, my phone beeps in my pocket. I take it out and look at the screen. *Fertile day*, my app tells me. *Have sex.*

I'd forgotten that my fertile window was coming up. I thought James looked at me awkwardly last night when I told him I was going on this spur-of-the-moment trip. We've got only two more cycles before my next dive. Still, not having to do it today is a bit of a relief.

There are no weird noises coming from downstairs, thank goodness. Dad sleeps in a room off the lounge these days. It used to be the dining room when I was a kid. When I was little, my dad and I used to play a thing we called "pillow talk." I'd lie by the headboard of his bed, and he would climb under the covers, saying, "Cor, I'm whacked. Time for some shut-eye." He'd make this big show of settling down for the night, and then he'd lie back on me as I pretended to be his pillow. I'd let him "fall asleep" for a few moments, and then I'd say something and laugh, and he would look around in shock, going: "What? Who said that? It sounded like it was coming from my . . . my *pillow*! But it can't be. Pillows don't talk!" He'd reach behind his head and pretend to plump me up, making me laugh even more, and the cycle would go on and on. Back then, Dad slept only three or four hours a night.

I put my mum's folder on the floor and lie back. *Have sex*, my phone tells me again, and I switch off the reminder. I Google pictures of Irish wolfhounds for a while. Maybe a second dog is what I need. Then, I check my emails. Spam from an estate agent, a weekly fitness report from MapMyRun, and then this: an email from the Mars Project. The subject heading is "Your entry."

"Dear Ms. Solvig Dean . . . pleased to inform you . . . through to the next round of the contest . . . required to attend a conference day at Center Parcs in Sherwood Forest, Nottinghamshire . . ."

I drop my phone, as if it's scorching hot, and I look up at the ceiling, where glow-in-the-dark stars were once stuck. I'm not thinking about Irish wolfhounds or childhood games any more. I'm thinking about dark nebulae, giant voids, black holes.

17

"Are you sure you can handle this?" I ask James. "You could always go to the café and hang out with the kids."

"You're just nervous you won't be able to keep up with the robo-leg." James finishes attaching his running blade and gets out of the car.

"I'm talking about your heart, mate," I say, prodding him in the chest. "A couple of Parkruns here and there aren't exactly gonna prepare you for this."

"Pfft, it's a mere 17K," he retorts. "I'm worried about *you* because you're twice as likely to get blisters as me. Mate." He grabs his water bottle out of the trunk.

I bare my teeth at him, then put in my earphones and start running towards the coastal path. We leave Kynance Cove and head east towards Cadgwith. It's only May, but the sky is cloudless and blue. A perfect day to be out on the Lizard Peninsula. I'm glad James suggested it. His running prosthesis has been gathering dust since Christmas, but now he's getting active to boost our chances of conception. It's good to see him being physical. I feel more attracted to him when he exercises.

The Lizard Peninsula is a Cornwall Area of Outstanding Natural Beauty. This part of the county really gets James going. On the way over here, he explained to me that the rocks on the peninsula are made of oceanic crust.

"Speaking of crusts," I replied, "let's get pizza tonight."

James slowed to take a bend in the road. "The word *pizza* is over a thousand years old," he pontificated.

I've downloaded a podcast to listen to on today's run. It's part of a science series run by two guys in Colorado. This episode is called "Women in Space." I haven't listened to any of the other episodes in this series before, but there are some intriguing titles such as: "How to Grow Skin" and "The Truth about Crows."

"Hey, Elijah," says a guy in my earphones. I take a quick look behind me. James gives me a wave. I increase my pace.

"Good to see you again, Powell."

Irritatingly, Elijah and Powell start talking about their weekends, and this goes on for some time. To summarise: Elijah went to a flea market with his wife, but they didn't buy anything. Powell went to a gig and drank too many Keystone Ices. Today Elijah and Powell are drinking Cougar Pale Ale, as supplied by Elijah, whose house they are recording in.

"Let's talk about women in space," says Elijah, cutting short Powell's story about where he woke up after the gig.

"Oh right, that's what we're talking about," laughs Powell, taking an audible gulp of beer. "Well, Colorado is an aerospace mecca, so we had to talk about this stuff at some point, right?

And we thought we'd give it a twist by talking about *women* in space."

"The first woman in space was the Soviet cosmonaut Valentina Tereshkova," says Elijah. "She orbited the earth forty-eight times in 1963."

"It was a man who came up with the idea of sending a woman to space, right?" Powell chimes in. He then affects a bad Russian accent: "Sergey Korolyov."

"That's right. And there were these super-strict criteria. The women had to be skydivers, under thirty, less than five foot seven, under 154 pounds . . ."

"That's standard practise for astronauts anyway, isn't it? I'm pretty sure you have to be, like, under two hundred pounds to get into NASA."

Elijah laughs. "There go my hopes and dreams!"

"You and me both, buddy."

"Anyway, Tereshkova logged more flight time than all the American astronauts who'd flown before her put together."

"Yeah, and everyone was like, 'That was cool.' But then no women went to space for nineteen years after that."

"The second one to go was Russian again, I think?"

This is an even more difficult run than I'd anticipated. The coastal path is narrow and uneven. I really hope James is all right.

On the podcast, Elijah and Powell have started talking about American women in space. Apparently, the US has sent up forty females since 1983. My mum died in December 1983, so she'd have been alive to witness Sally Ride, the first American woman, go up in June of that year.

Elijah talks about female astronauts from all sorts of other places: Japan, China, Italy, South Korea. And one from Britain too. Helen Sharman got the job after responding to a radio advertisement. At the time, she was working for Mars, the confectioners. Her job involved studying the physical and chemical properties of chocolate. She beat thirteen thousand other applicants, and off she went to a Soviet space station. "From Mars to *Mir*," jokes Elijah.

Powell has been quiet for some time. "Elijah," he says now, "let's talk about sexism."

"Sure," Elijah replies. Am I imagining irritation in his voice? "Female astronauts, who the media once dubbed 'astronettes,' have had to deal with a lot of prejudice, particularly in the early days of space travel. Jerrie Cobb, who was part of Mercury 13—"

"Mercury 13 was a group of thirteen American women who underwent many of the same tests as the men in Project Mercury, right?"

"Correct."

"But NASA cancelled the women's programme and didn't select any of them to go to space."

"Jerrie Cobb," continues Elijah, "passed all three phases of her tests, ranking her in the top 2 percent of all astronaut candidates of both sexes. During this gruelling process, whenever the press interviewed her, they asked her about cooking. And before Shannon Lucid spent 188 days in space, she was quizzed about how her children would handle her being away for so long."

"It is a weird one, though," interjects Powell. "I don't know how I would've felt having my mom blast off to space when I was a kid."

"What about your dad?" asks Elijah.

"Well, my dad was never around."

There's a pause before Elijah goes on to list several well-known male astronauts with families. Alan Shepard's three kids frequently attended NASA events. John Young had two wives and two children. Buzz Aldrin had three wives and three children.

I've got to go to a conference in Nottinghamshire for the next round of the competition. I've told James I've got a dive coming up in Liverpool, that I'll be cleaning out a reservoir.

My gaze wanders up towards the sky. It's not selfish to want to see what's out there, is it? Kids may never happen, after all. It's only sensible to have a plan B. Even if I do get pregnant, the first crew isn't due to set off until 2030. If I give birth next year, she'll reach double figures by the time I'm due to leave. Surely I'll have done all the important groundwork by then? And we could still communicate regularly. It takes about twenty minutes for a message to travel back to Earth from Mars. A bit slower than ideal, but at least I wouldn't have my helium voice. And a lagging conversation could teach my child a lot about the virtues of patience.

As for James and I . . . well, it's a lot like going for this run. I'm doing my thing, he's doing his. We're together, but that doesn't mean we have to be joined at the hip. Who wouldn't want a cosmic girlfriend? Also, and this is the main thing: *As if I'm going to win the competition! As if I'll ever go to Mars! Pigs might fly!*

I'm looking so far into the distance that I trip and fall onto my hands and knees. My palms are flecked with rock dust: an inverse night sky.

18

As I switch off the car engine, I have to remind myself to breathe. *One small step for man*, I think, as my feet hit the tarmac.

I think I've always underestimated Center Parcs. Calling it a "holiday village" conjures a whole host of nightmarish images. Gurning families, decaying chalets, a theme-park-sized swimming pool, and water slides as tall as skyscrapers. But this Center Parcs is located in Sherwood Forest. The ancient woodland is expansive and peaceful, and the living accommodation looks classy: honey-coloured wooden cabins, with big windows and clean lines.

I take my rucksack out of the trunk and head towards Lodge 355. Inside, it's basically an IKEA showroom. There's an angular grey sofa with a matching footstool. On the wall is a black-and-white print of a woodland scene. Off to the right is the kitchen area, full of shiny white cupboards and wipe-clean surfaces. The sort of person who might live in a place like this is a single, organised businesswoman, with a name like Jenny.

Jenny wouldn't put her bags down by the door. She'd take them into the bedroom and put her clothes straight into the wardrobe, so that's what I'm going to do.

The bedroom is a study in maroon. Maroon walls, maroon bedcovers, maroon lamp. *Maroon* is a word I haven't thought about for a very long time. Maroon is Jenny's favourite colour. It hides stains, while adding a touch of sophistication.

I put my rucksack on the bed, chastising myself for not owning more elegant baggage. Then I take out my clothes and hang each crumpled item in the wardrobe.

Next, I plonk the supplies I picked up on the way here on the kitchen counter: a bottle of red wine, half a baguette, and a packet of salami. This is perfect. A simple charcuterie. Jenny would approve. I prepare my food slowly, enjoying opening and closing cupboards, discovering the crockery and cutlery that is to be mine for the next two days. The plates are white and round as full moons, fecund with possibilities.

I take my meal to the sofa. This is such a small thing, to be here in Center Parcs with a salami sandwich and a glass of wine, but the adrenaline is coursing through my bloodstream. I feel as though someone is filming me for a documentary about my life. As though I am about to achieve something so great, so momentous, that every boring thing I have ever done suddenly has great significance.

"What was she doing the day before her future was decided?" people will ask. "Sitting on the sofa eating a sandwich," others will answer. There will be a collective gasp.

I switch on the TV and flick through a few channels. *Take Me Out. Four in a Bed. The Secret Life of the Zoo.* I take a swig of red wine—my first taste of alcohol in three months—and briefly quiz myself. First man in space? Yuri Gagarin. First to set foot on the moon? Everyone knows that. Last to set foot on the moon? Damn it, I've forgotten.

"The pygmy marmoset can rotate its head up to 180 degrees," an earnest young zookeeper says straight to the camera. I switch off the telly.

I open Spotify on my phone and type *Mars* into the search bar. There it is: "Mars, the Bringer of War" by Gustav Holst. I hear the urgent plucking of strings and I increase the volume. I imagine myself floating up, up, out of Jenny's skin, and out of Sherwood Forest.

I pick up my phone and text a single word to James: *Hope*.

19

What do you mean? That was his first reply, but there were others.

How was your journey?

Having fun in Liverpool?

Fuck, Solvig. Pick up your phone.

I've completely forgotten what my text message meant. Something highly profound and utterly stupid, no doubt. As I trek towards the conference centre, I manage to cobble together a reply: *Meant to say: hope you're having a good evening. Oops! Talk later.*

It's 7:30 a.m. and I didn't bring anything with me for breakfast. I've cleaned my teeth, but my mouth still tastes sour. The wine went to my head fast. I ended up working my way through Holst's entire *Planets* suite. I was laughing by the time I got to "Jupiter, the Bringer of Jollity," but then, halfway through "Saturn, the Bringer of Old Age," I became maudlin. If only I hadn't polished off that whole bottle, I could have gone for a run this morning. There are plenty of healthy people out here, jogging around the forest trails.

It's hard to get my head around being in a holiday park for such a serious occasion. I wonder why the organisers chose this place. I've seen the Center Parcs adverts enough times to know that there's a gigantic water slide here. I can't help but picture the conference involving us having to fling ourselves down the slide one by one, shouting: "To infinity and beyond!" I do know that Center Parcs was founded in the Netherlands, same as the Mars Project. I wonder if it was picked for that reason, or just because it's a convenient location. The ancient landscape of Sherwood Forest feels apt, in any case. It has areas of woodland dating back to the Ice Age. Funny to think about space as an ancient landscape. Feels like it's the future, even if everything we can see out there—all of it—has already happened.

I walk past the inexplicably French "Jardin des Sports" and towards the "Subtropical Swimming Paradise." In the middle of the park, I spot a sign with the least exotic of all the place names on it: "The Venue." The building ahead is wooden and angular, in keeping with the rest of the architecture at Center Parcs. However, other places I've passed have been decorated with colourful canopies and bright outdoor furniture. This place has none of that stuff. It means business.

I have one last attempt at smoothing out the creases of my outfit, and head towards the entrance.

Outside, a few people are smoking. Are any of them fellow space hopefuls? If so, are they trying to quit, or will they break the habit once their seats to Mars are secured? Perhaps their plan is to go cold turkey at lift-off. I used to know a saturation diver called Bill who smoked twenty cigarettes a day. He had to go without them every time he went into the chamber. "Don't do me no harm," Bill would say, shrugging his broad shoulders, but we could see him, jiggling his legs up and down, sticking on patch after patch, counting down the days until he was set free. Last I heard he'd given up diving and had become a children's entertainer.

As soon as I enter the building, I see a metal stand with a piece of A4 in its frame, displaying the words "Mars Conference." I'm tempted to pull out my phone and take a picture, but I hear voices close behind me.

A woman says: "It was either this or go and work for Elon Musk in LA."

A man replies: "Yup. Yup. Yup. I know what you mean."

I walk briskly in the direction of the arrow until I come to a table full of badges.

"Name," says a man in a tweed jacket.

I tell him what he wants to hear, and he hands me a badge.

"Cloakroom on your left. Refreshments yonder."

Some people might call this man abrupt, but I admire his efficiency. Rather than waste his time with words, I thank him with a nod and head for the snacks.

I'd been half expecting space food to be served here: tubes of applesauce or freeze-dried eggs. I've heard that NASA is currently developing 3D-printed food. A 3D-printed fry-up would sort my hangover right out. Still, a croissant and coffee will suffice. I help myself, then find a chair. The coffee tastes okay. Coffee is normally a reliable first indicator. If the coffee's good, you can be optimistic about the rest.

There must be about fifty of us in the foyer so far. A few look as if they're about to be interviewed for slick finance jobs.

Others don't. I can count eight NASA T-shirts from where I'm sitting. Someone has a Ziggy Stardust flash over his right eye, and there are a couple of steampunks over in the corner, wearing trench coats, top hats, pocket watches, and mechanical accessories. I look down at my boring outfit and wonder if the mundane, practical look might be exactly what the organisers are after.

The male-female split is roughly fifty-fifty. That sort of thing shouldn't be a shock, but perhaps because I'm the only woman on my dive team, I mistakenly assumed I was going to be outnumbered here too. Normally it spurs me on, being among men, feeling like I have to prove myself. Here, there's no way I can coast through to the next round of the contest by being "the token woman." I need to find a way to stand out.

There's a red-haired woman picking up a *pain au chocolat* at the refreshments table who's clearly pregnant. Must be at least seven or eight months gone. She's wearing a floral dress, and she looks very feminine and, frankly, very out of place. I wonder if she's an administrator or one of the speakers. I blush as she looks over in my direction, but she hasn't caught me staring. She's spotted the empty seat beside me, and heads over. We eat our pastries side by side, and I focus on other things: the teenage girl manning the coffee machine, the various levels of polish on delegates' shoes, the faux chandelier above the refreshments table.

After a few minutes, the door to the Major Oak Suite opens. I want to make sure I get a good seat, so I put down my empty cup and plate, wipe my greasy hands on my trousers, and head in.

The room is impersonal: rows of black chairs facing a stage, on which there is a podium, a screen, and a large speaker system. No space paraphernalia. No to-scale model of the pod that the first humans on Mars will be residing in. Nothing to give away the momentous nature of today's event, other than another piece of A4 paper, with "Mars Conference" printed across the middle of it in black ink.

I opt for the third row: keen, without being too eager. Two young women in tinfoil hats make a big fuss of squeezing past me, irritated that I've picked an aisle seat. I don't really care. I'm damned if two girls wearing tinfoil are going to have a better view than I am.

One of the final stragglers to enter the room is the pregnant woman. She takes a seat at the front.

There's a crackle on the speakers, and Bowie's "Life on Mars?" begins to play. Everyone falls silent, as if we're at church listening to the organ while we wait for the coffin to be carried in. Bowie sings to us about sunken dreams and saddening bores, and then, as the music dies down, I hear the woman in the tinfoil hat next to me hiss to her companion: "As a matter of fact, that song has nothing to do with Mars." I miss her friend's response, because at this moment, a woman in a beige trouser suit walks down the aisle towards the podium.

"Good morning, everyone," she says. There's a twinge of a foreign accent. She looks in her midforties, with jaw-length hair and an extreme side-parting: professional and futuristic. As she runs her gaze over the audience, it feels as though she's appraising each and every one of us. I sit up straighter.

"I'm Fabienne Baas, head recruiter for the Mars Project."

It's so quiet I hear myself swallow.

"During this morning's session," Fabienne says, "I'm going to give you some crucial information. Then, this afternoon, we'll split you into groups and observe you." She tucks her hair behind her ears. Her expression changes from serious to excited. Or at least a well-rehearsed impression of someone who is excited. "Let's get straight to it. Who here wants to live on Mars?"

As if we have been primed by a TV producer for a live show, we clap and cheer. The cheering is like rain after a humid day. Too sudden, too strong, but it clears some of the tension in the air. I notice that the pregnant woman in the front row is whooping.

"Good. That's great." Fabienne's smile is starting to look genuine. "It's wonderful to see so many of you here in the Major Oak Suite. I am reliably informed that this room is named after Robin Hood's hideout. For the purposes of today, though, it's more like the Major *Tom* suite, don't you agree?"

Another round of applause.

Fabienne switches on the screen behind her. We might be planning the most advanced interplanetary expedition ever attempted by the human race, but we're still at the evolutionary stage where PowerPoint presentations are the done thing.

"Here you can see a timeline for the project." Fabienne points at the screen. There's an arrow running from left to right. Above the start of the arrow, it says "Now." At the end, it says "2030." There are five other points marked along the way:

- 2020 - Select crew
- 2021 - Train crew
- 2025 - Communications mission
- 2027 - Cargo mission
- 2028 - Outpost preparation

Fabienne tells us that there is a lot to do before we are ready to colonise Mars. We need to send out a rover to prepare the outpost, and communication satellites to enable contact with Earth. We'll need living units, as well as support units containing air, water, and food. Fabienne's voice is calm and reassuring, and several people nod as she speaks. My guess is that they're nodding less out of comprehension than relief. Relief that someone has thought this thing through.

Reaching the end of the timeline, Fabienne points at the final date. "This is the big one," she says. "In 2030, Mars will be inhabited."

Several people fidget, me included.

"As you probably know, the planets need to be properly aligned, so there is only one launch window to Mars every twenty-six months. That's when Mars is at its closest point to Earth, known as the *perigee*." A PowerPoint slide pops up with the word *PERIGEE* in capital letters. It's quickly replaced by a picture of a spacecraft that looks a bit like a giant battery pack. "This," says Fabienne, pointing at the slide, "is how you'll be getting there."

She pauses. "That's right—I said 'you.' Because it could be you, or you, or *you*." She points at specific people in the audience, and I'm annoyed that on the third "you" she points at the girl in the tinfoil hat next to me.

Fabienne raises a finger to her lips, hushing the whispering in the room. "Now listen," she says. "You're probably wondering what kind of candidates we're looking for. Well, if you're serious about taking part in this mission, you'll need to be . . ." An acrostic appears behind her:

Mars-obsessed
Ambitious
Resilient
Trusting/trustworthy
Inquisitive
Adaptable
Nice
Sense of humour

"That's right, you need to be Martians!" Fabienne says this as if she's just delivered her coup de grâce. She then talks us through each of the qualities listed on the screen.

When she reaches the final line on the acrostic, she announces: "And now we come to the big one. If you want to go to Mars, you've got to have a sense of humour." For some reason, everyone laughs when she says this. Are we laughing at the notion of jokes in general? Do I lack a sense of humour because I can't understand what's so funny?

20

Honestly though, what makes me laugh?

There was that biology lesson at school, where we learnt the scientific name for a European badger: *Meles meles.* My friend Alana and I got the giggles. It was the repetition that got to us. When the teacher told us that the name of one of the badger subspecies was *Meles meles meles,* we were beside ourselves. Kept daring each other to try and say *meles* three times in a row without laughing. These days, I think I could say *meles* indefinitely.

I step out into the midday sun, looking for a place to eat lunch. My brow is furrowed. What's my sense of humour like? Hidden under a mass of anxiety.

The steampunks are sitting at a picnic table, along with a couple of people in suits. One woman's jacket has shoulder pads. Near a sign saying "Dog Exercise Area," I spot the pregnant woman. She's perched on a tree stump. I find myself gravitating towards her.

"Mind if I join you?"

"Mmm, please." She wipes sandwich crumbs from the corner of her mouth.

I sit on the stump too and say: "Nice to get a bit of fresh air." I feel instantly silly. I'm here because I want to live on Mars for the rest of my life, never again feeling the wind in my hair, or a lick of breeze on my cheek.

The woman laughs, and I wonder if that means I just made a joke. "It's all getting a teensy bit intense in there, isn't it?"

"It's good to get a breather from the Bowie stuff for five minutes," I say. A small thrill runs through me for daring to come so close to a criticism.

The woman strokes a strand of hair away from her face. Her eyes are green, and her features are unapologetic. It could be because she's expecting a baby. A pregnant belly seems to me to be the greatest expression of female confidence there is. Growing something so huge and extraordinary before everyone's eyes.

"Thirty-two weeks tomorrow," says the woman. She's caught me staring. "Not too much longer now. Have you got kids?"

"No, not yet." My cheeks flush. Even saying that—"not yet"—makes me feel strange. The idea that I could be planning to do something as radical as become a mother seems so entitled. I think I'm good enough for *that*, do I? And—at the same time—I reckon I've got what it takes to be an astronaut? Wow. I must really rate myself. I pick up a sandwich triangle.

"Evelyn," she says, giving her name badge a quick glance. "Evie."

I'm eating, so I point at my chest.

"Solvig," she says. "Scandinavian heritage?"

I put my hand to my mouth to conceal the food I'm still chewing. "My mum just liked the name. Said it reminded her of a bowl of soup."

Evie laughs. I made another joke by accident. "It's a Norse name," Evie tells me. "Something to do with the sun. My husband would be able to tell you more about that. He's a medieval studies professor."

"What is it you do?" I ask.

"I'm a forensic botanist in Birmingham. Previously I worked in biotechnology, at a germplasm resources lab."

I raise my eyebrows, as if I have not only understood the information but also found it compelling. I reach for another sandwich triangle. "What does being a forensic botanist entail?" I venture.

"Well, quite!" She gives me a conspiratorial look. "It's a relatively new discipline. There are different branches to it. I'm involved in palynology. That's the study of pollen. If there's a rare plant growing near the scene of a murder, for example, then pollen presence on the suspect can provide a strong case for prosecution." She pauses. "My botanical skills could be used differently on Mars. That's where the biotech comes in. I've created a synthetic Martian soil in my greenhouse at home. Not a perfect replica, I grant you, but I'm using it to develop plants that are well suited to the Martian environment. I'm getting some promising results with radishes. Good news for space tacos! Anyway, listen to me rabbiting on. What about you, Solvig?"

For a moment, a nasty thought creeps into my mind: maybe Evie will die in childbirth, eliminating her from the competition.

"I'm a saturation diver," I say. "North Sea–based. Oil stuff." I decide to say something self-deprecating about my job, as a form of self-punishment, something about how there's no oil in space, but then I remember that there is. Instead, I say piteously: "Pollen is more interesting than oil."

"A saturation diver?" Evie says. "How marvellous."

Before I have the chance to denigrate myself any further, I'm saved by a bichon frise, who bounds over and starts sniffing my paper plate, trying to snatch up my final piece of ham and cheese sandwich. I jerk away the plate but give the dog a pat on the head as consolation. It's a shame Cola isn't here. He'd love to lollop around a place like this, but the journey would literally kill him. At least he'll be dead by 2030, so I won't have to worry about leaving him behind.

I hear shrieking over by the picnic table and see that the steampunks are sharing some moment of great hilarity with the girls in tinfoil.

"Do you have to be crazy to want to go on a mission like this?" I ask Evie.

She follows my gaze. "Was Ranulph Fiennes crazy when he set off for the North Pole? I mean, I suppose he's a bad example, because he cut his own frostbitten fingertips off with a fretsaw. Imagine that!" Evie winces and places her hands protectively over her stomach. "Solvig: if craziness means being brave and ambitious and spirited and even a little foolish, then yes, we *are* crazy to have applied for a mission like this. But thank God for insanity."

"He cut off his own fingertips," I say, crossing my arms.

"Look, when people started volunteering for the first manned space missions, everyone thought they must be suicidal or mentally ill. Or trying to escape some darkness within themselves."

My skin prickles.

•

"Okay, guys. Listen up. This is where things get serious."

A man in a red cap is standing at the front of the room. His name, which he's told us three times, is Brodie. He's got an English accent but with American intonations, as though he's binge-watched too many episodes of *Friends*.

"This afternoon's activities are going to last two hours, okay? You'll be working with the people at your table." There are six tables in here. Ours has five women and two men at it. I was hoping that Evie would be in here too, but she's not.

"You've been assigned groups randomly, so no ulterior motives. I'll be making notes while you're doing the exercises. Make sure I can see your name badges, okay?"

As he speaks, Brodie strides around the room, never quite making eye contact with us, glancing furtively at the tables, the backs of our chairs, our jumpers. He's desperate to be comfortable in this environment, and we're desperate for him to be comfortable too. Unfortunately, he's beginning to sweat. The sweat is gathering beneath the peak of his cap.

"The first exercise of the afternoon," Brodie explains, "is a humorous twist on the classic balloon debate." He freezes and points at the ceiling with a terrified expression. "Beware!"

Startled, I follow his gaze. I see an air-conditioning unit and a strip of fluorescent lighting.

"The transit vehicle that you and your group are travelling on is about to crash," Brodie says.

I exhale, realising that we are only in imaginary peril. Some people laugh. I laugh too, in case I'm somehow being monitored.

"The only way to avoid certain death is to lighten your vehicle's load. That means throwing people out of the craft, to wither and die in the infinite void." Brodie mimes the discarding of a human body as if pitching slop out of a window. "The vehicle will only comfortably hold four, so you're going to need to lose three people. Or four, if you're at the table of eight. Think about what skills everyone in your team has to offer. Remember: you're going to be the first four people colonising a new planet. What's the best combination you can come up with, to give you a fighting chance of making it on Mars?" Brodie twirls his finger as if he's a conductor, instructing his orchestra to start playing. "Twenty minutes. Then report back."

I once read a *Mental Floss* article about what happens if you suddenly find you have been spewed out into space without adequate protection. You will suffer horrific sunburn, while at the same time being subjected to an agonising chill. You will fill up with gas bubbles and double in size. The moisture on your eyes and in your mouth will boil. If you hold your breath, your lungs will rupture. If you don't, you'll suffocate.

I turn to the people at my table, scanning name badges. Who do I want to kill? There's a guy with a white goatee opposite me called Yuri. There's no way that's his real name. I instantly hate him. We should chuck him out first.

Before I have the chance to poison the group against him, the woman on Yuri's left, Carol, who has short grey hair and a kind face, takes a deep breath and says: "I volunteer to die."

What? Is this how we're meant to play the game? The people who are willing to sacrifice themselves are the ones who get to take part in the most ambitious space project known to man?

Yuri looks at Carol, takes her hand in his, and says, "I also volunteer to die."

Bloody hell. At this rate, we'll have nobody left.

I lean forwards and lock eyes with Yuri. "I'd very much like to stay on the vehicle," I declare forcefully. "I want to live."

A couple of people at the table fidget, and then, shame-faced, they murmur: "Me too."

"Excellent," I say. "Well, let's see who'd work best with me." With those words, I've become the leader.

Yuri and Carol remain eerily quiet throughout the ensuing conversation, no doubt feeling that their martyrdom has already proved far more than words ever could. I, on the other hand, become supremely, uncharacteristically loud. I use words like *determine* and *subset* and *perfunctory*. When Brodie comes over with a clipboard to observe us, I even make a joke.

"You think we need a chef on Mars?" I say to Angelika, the woman next to me. "Your food had better be out of this world!"

Brodie, whose cap says "You rocket" above the peak, laughs. After he's finished laughing, I catch him looking at my name badge. Oh yes. I can do this.

After Brodie walks away, I turn to Raissa, the one person in our group who hasn't said anything yet. "What about you? What do you do?"

"I write haikus," she replies shyly.

"You're in," I tell her.

At the end of the exercise, we've whittled our crew down to a robust four. I'm on the crew, naturally, and there's also: Katie (an endocrinologist), Landon (a molecular biochemist), and Raissa (a poet). Rejected are Angelika (a chef), Carol (a Christian missionary), and Yuri (a painter).

"Interesting choice," says Brodie when it's our turn to report back to the room. "What made you decide to take the poet?"

Raissa bites her lip and I speak for her. "It was a toss-up between taking her or a rocket scientist," I say. "Just kidding."

Everyone chuckles. I'm really getting the hang of this.

Now, I clear my throat. I tell Brodie that we decided it was important that we document such a momentous occasion. I tell Brodie that nobody knows exactly what's going to happen when we get to Mars. I tell Brodie that it's vital that such a significant milestone for the human race be communicated *with heart*.

Brodie holds out his clipboard, and he writes something down, slowly and deliberately.

"Time for the next activity," he says at last. "This one's called 'The Point of No Return.'"

21

As I'm about to break free of the conference room, Brodie calls out: "Don't forget to line up in the foyer for a photograph!"

"What's the photograph for?" I ask the girl filing out of the room ahead of me.

"Apparently, they're going to put our pictures online; then the public have to vote for who they like the best."

"Excuse me?"

"That's how they get it down to a shortlist of one hundred. It's going to be high-key amazing." The girl looks barely eighteen. She's wearing false eyelashes.

"So, our success in this competition is based on a photograph?"

"Lol," says the girl. "Not just our pictures. They're putting up our essays too."

"Jesus."

The girl takes a lip gloss out of her pocket. "You coming to the activity centre after this?" she asks as we shuffle forwards. "A group of us are going to Laser Combat."

"Maybe," I lie.

Naturally, the photographer is incredibly photogenic. She's wearing leggings and a vintage jumper, looks about twenty-five, and has poker-straight hair. "Stand here please," she instructs me through a lens.

I imagine her uploading my image onto her computer later tonight. She's surrounded by mid-century modern furniture and sampling a chilled white wine as she clones bits of my "good skin" from anywhere she can find it, then pastes it liberally over my wrinkles, eye bags, moustache hair.

"It would be great if you could smile," she says. "Think about how much you want to go to outer space."

Maybe this trick has been working on some of the others, but I feel like a patronised child. *How much I want to go to outer space?* This isn't a joke. I'm not a five-year-old lying under a rocket-themed duvet cover, dreaming of becoming the next Neil Armstrong. This is my Big Dream. The only thing I want in life.

Oh no.

This is the only thing I want.

"Never mind," says the photographer. "That'll do."

I rub my temples and head for the exit. It's only 4:30. I don't really need to stay here an extra night. I could be home by 1:00 a.m. I call James as I walk through the forest.

"What are you up to?" I ask. I'm supposed to be on a regular diving job, not a sat dive, so thank heavens I don't have to fake a high-pitched voice.

"Waiting on my last customer. A Polynesian sea turtle."

"You're giving a turtle a tattoo. Ha."

"How's Liverpool?"

I look around me, at the log cabins, dog exercise areas, and play parks. "Busy, but good," I say. I'm walking up a path that runs alongside a lake. "Water stuff is going well." "Water stuff"? Can't I bring myself to use the word *diving*?

"I'm looking forward to seeing you tomorrow," says James.

"Hope Cola's behaving."

"I'm sorry we didn't get more time to talk after you started your, you know, your period. We'll get there, Solvig. It's a gamble. We've only got a 25 percent chance in any given month."

"Twenty-five seems high," I say, plucking a leaf off a bush. As it happens, I know that the figure is more like 10 percent for someone of my age, but even that feels high too.

"Better go," James says quickly. "I can see my customer heading up the street. Call me tonight if you have time. Anouk and I are taking Nike surfing after I'm done here. Good waves today."

"Right," I say. "Speak later, then." I hang up, feeling inexplicably annoyed that my boyfriend and best friend are going surfing together. And with a kid too. If James can't have a baby with me, then he's putting together a backup family.

Obviously, that's nonsense. Anouk is James's friend and physio. She was the one who encouraged him to get back into surfing after the accident, and even helped him source a custom-made wetsuit.

The crash happened six years ago. By the time I met James, he seemed like he'd come to terms with it. He told me it couldn't have been a more Cornish crash: he was meandering around a narrow country road, five miles per hour over the limit, when he came face-to-face with a combine harvester. The combine had broken down, but its lights weren't working. James swerved to avoid it and went face-first into a truck, which happened to be carrying St. Austell Brewery's signature Cornish pale ale, Tribute. The truck was barely dented. James's Mini crunched up like a used Coke can. James suffered a fractured pelvis, a shattered tibia and fibula, a torn artery, and three severed tendons.

Turns out, James's left calf had been home to his only tattoo: a crucifix. As a lapsed Catholic, James enjoys telling people that the car crash was God's revenge. Ink-free after the amputation, James decided he wanted a new tattoo. It was the first tattoo he ever drew himself: a three-toed sloth, the slowest mammal in the world. Underneath, the words "Steady does it."

I'm still holding the leaf, scrunched tightly in my fist. I let it fall to the ground.

·

I end up beneath the great glass dome of the Subtropical Swimming Paradise. There are palm trees and plastic chairs, and an entire clientele (apart from me) dressed in bathing gear.

I buy a pint of 6 percent hard cider from the poolside bar, then seek out the driest place to sit. The cider is vinegary and expensive, but it's good to have a drink. That's two days in a row I've had alcohol now. I can feel my fertility draining away with each mouthful.

A week ago, I might have told people I was desperate for a baby. Yesterday morning, I might even have said the same.

But how can you ever know for sure that you want to do something as huge as create a human? When I was a kid, I used to ask my dad how I'd know when I'd found the right person to settle down with for the rest of my life. "You'll just know," he'd say, with a mysterious wink. Well, I still don't know the answer to that question, let alone the one about having a baby. I think an easier question for me is whether I want to get pregnant. I mean, I don't look forward to being pregnant. But I know that I want to *get* pregnant. I can't bear not achieving my goals.

"Solvig, mind if I sit with you?"

It's Evie. Have I conjured her here by thinking about pregnancy? I shake my head. "Please."

She sits, catching her breath, and puts a blue Slush Puppie on the table. "How did your afternoon session go?"

"It was hard work," I say. "Demonstrating what a capable team worker I am. How fanatical I am about Mars. What an accomplished astronaut I'd make. While at the same time showing off my *smashing* sense of humour."

Evie laughs. "It was a bit like that, wasn't it?" She slips off a shoe and rubs her foot. "There was one young man in my group who I think would have gladly chucked everyone out of the rocket and flown to Mars all by himself."

I roll my eyes.

"Women," Evie says, chuckling, "they might be from Venus, but they belong on Mars." I can't help but notice that Evie looks at me when she says "women." For some reason, it feels good to be categorised.

"But how would we populate Mars?" I ask mischievously.

Evie fixes me with a puzzled expression, then imbibes Slush Puppie through a red straw.

"There'll be no *populating* up there, I'm afraid," she says. "I mean, technically, it's possible. The African clawed frog was proven to ovulate on the space shuttle *Endeavour*. And the pregnant rat that the Soviets took up gave birth afterwards. Offspring were a tad weak to begin with, but they soon caught up."

It's weird to hear a pregnant woman talking like this, in such clinical terms. I wonder if Evie ever thinks of the baby she is carrying as her "offspring."

"The biggest challenge is radiation," she continues. "If there's enough of a shield in the living quarters, that may prevent damage to developing foetuses. But as of yet, we haven't witnessed human gestation in space, let alone on a new planet, so . . . we'll see."

"You know a lot about this," I say.

"If you've got the urge to bear children, Solvig, my advice is that you deal with that urge now."

I hide behind my pint glass.

Evie runs her fingers over her stomach, causing the floral print to stretch, taut, over her bump. She leans forward conspiratorially. "When did you first know? You know, that you wanted to go?"

"Probably not long after my mum died," I reply, my demeanour not as cool as I'd like.

"Oh, Solvig."

"I used to sit on the edge of my bed, aged three or four, looking out of my window." I mime this action by looking up at the dome above us. "I was so sure she was up there. In the sky."

"That's beautiful." It looks like Evie might be about to cry. "It's how I want my children to feel. If I go. I want them to think of me every time they look up. The sky is everywhere, so I'll always be with them."

It surprises me that Evie is already a parent. I have so many questions. *How many children do you have? Do you feel guilty at the thought of leaving them behind? Did you always know, for sure, that you wanted them in the first place? Do you ever feel like a bad person?* Instead, all I can muster is: "Evie, do you want another drink?"

Evie studies her Slush Puppie and sticks out her tongue. It's ultramarine. She laughs. "My eldest boy's favourite," she said. "He might be able to have two in a row, but I can't even finish one."

"He must be very proud of you," I say quietly.

Evie pushes the cup away. "He hasn't handled this too well, to be honest. Ever since I entered the competition, he's spent every evening up in his room, playing *Minecraft*. He's building a to-scale model of the Eiffel Tower. Made of ice."

"I'm sorry."

"The twins are a couple of years younger than Leo. They're thrilled. They think I'm Flash Gordon. 'Mummy's going to live in space!' I think their concept of forever only runs to next week."

"So many kids."

"Yes," laughs Evie. "So many kids."

"And what about your husband?" I ask. "You did say you were married, didn't you?"

Evie's expression softens. "Cedric was the one who suggested I do this."

"Really?"

"He heard a segment on the *Today* programme and emailed me a link to the Mars Project website straight afterwards. He knows how much this opportunity means to me. I imagine he was hoping I'd laugh it off. But it's just a case of making it work long-distance, isn't it?"

I look deep into my empty pint glass. "Making it work. Yeah."

"I'm sure now he's got used to the idea he's proud . . . thrilled . . . happy."

I can't resist smiling. Evie is referencing Rene Carpenter, the American astronaut Scott Carpenter's first wife. In interviews, she was repeatedly asked how she felt about her husband being "blasted into space," and those three words became her stock reply. Who knows what really lurked behind those adjectives?

Evie reaches for my hand and strokes my knuckles. "It's been so good to meet you today, Solvig." She pauses. "I haven't been on an adventure like this for so long."

I give her hand a soft squeeze. "It's been like that for me too. An adventure."

"Look," says Evie, wiping her eyes. "Why don't we get out of here? This isn't the celebratory atmosphere I was hoping for. We might be living on another planet soon, for heaven's sake! Let's not waste our time sitting beside a pool we're not even swimming in."

"Where do you suggest we go?"

"Back to my chalet," Evie says, and there's something about her expression that I like very much.

22

"Sorry I don't have any alcohol," says Evie, reaching into a shiny white cupboard. "I've got some rather potent sleepy tea if that does it for you?"

I inwardly lament not picking something up on the way. "Sleepy tea sounds fine."

Evie sorts the drinks and I sit down. Although her lodge is in a different area of the park—an area called Birch, not Willow—it's exactly the same as mine, right down to the black-and-white woodland scene on the wall. Because the lay-out is so familiar, I feel strangely at home. I put my feet up on the coffee table and sit back, closing my eyes.

"I can't wait to push this little blighter out and have a glass of champagne," Evie calls, above the noise of the kettle. "And a big platter of soft cheese. Six pregnancies later, that's far too many years of my life without brie."

"Why can't you eat brie?"

"Oh, some people do," Evie says, putting two identical black mugs on the table and rubbing her lower back before she sits. "Risk of listeria is low, but it's there. Same with deli meats and smoked salmon. I'm probably a worrywart, but after two losses, I'd rather not take the gamble."

Losses? Is Evie talking about miscarriages? It's so odd to hear them described like that. People lose their keys. Their glasses. Their wallet. I should express sympathy, but I don't know how. *Sorry for your losses.* That can't be right.

"Anyway," says Evie, putting her feet up next to mine. "I want to know more about you. Tell me everything."

"Everything? Well, I'm a diver. You know that."

"And your husband?"

"Oh, we're not married." My eternity ring catches my eye. I turn the half of the ring that's studded with diamonds face down, so that the gems are in my palm.

"And how does he feel about this?" She motions around the room. Presumably she's talking about more than Center Parcs; she's talking about the entire cosmos.

"He's okay," I reply, lightly touching the tip of my nose. Then I let my hands rest in my lap. "Evie," I mumble. "I haven't told him."

Evie grips my arm. "That's understandable, you know. It's a big thing. A humongous thing. It takes a certain type of partner to be able to get something like that."

"And your partner?" I ask. "You said he was the one who told you about the competition. Does he get it?"

"Cedric . . ." She picks up her mug from the coffee table, drumming her fingers on the ceramic. Her wedding ring clinks against it. "Cedric is a rare bird. He wasn't my professor at university, but he was working there while I was a student. There's a twenty-year age gap. I think that's helped us maintain a certain distance." She pauses. "This is going to sound like such a Cedric thing to say, but the word *distance* has such negative connotations. Why should it, though? It's merely the gap between two points."

I find myself looking into her mug, at the dark liquid contained within.

"Cedric and I have always enjoyed our own space. We've worked hard to maintain it. I mean, we're very close in some ways. We have three kids, and a fourth on the way. It'd be impossible to keep each other at arm's length all the time. We wouldn't want that. The emotional proximity is there, and often the physical too. But we're still open, still free." She turns to me. "Do you understand what I'm saying?"

I blink. "I think so."

"We're complicated creatures, Solvig," says Evie. "We need to be free to figure ourselves out."

"Have you?" I ask, drinking a mouthful of tea. Tastes of marshmallow and violets. "Figured yourself out?"

"Well, now there's the question." Evie smiles. Two dimples appear on her chin. "It's an ongoing project," she says. "Applying to go to Mars is part of that project. And so is sitting here now, being with you."

That phrase: "being with you." She could have said "talking to you," but she's acknowledging that we're in the same place. No distance.

"I like the sound of your life," I tell Evie.

"Yours sounds exciting," Evie responds. "Going off on your dives, getting away from it all."

I bite my lip. "Do you ever regret having children?"

Evie looks down. "It's draining playing host to someone else the whole time. Giving my babies everything I've got: my heart, my soul, my *nutrients*. What I wouldn't give for a day in your body, Solvig. A body that's only ever belonged to you. Full of edges and borders and definites. Those definites left my body a long time ago."

"But . . . you've chosen to have a large family?"

"Oh yes, I love being around young people. They fill me with hope for the future. But I do miss those sexy definites."

I put my mug down on the table a little too heavily, then jump up from the sofa. I should go. "Um," I say.

"Solvig, are you okay?" Evie stands too.

"Um," I say again.

"What is it, Solvig?"

Timidly, I ask: "Can I touch your bump?"

Evie takes a step forward. "Of course you can."

It takes a long time for my fingers to make contact, but eventually, I place my hands flat against Evie's belly, as if warming my palms before a fire. I'm shocked by how muscular it feels. "Wow," I whisper. "You made that."

Evie breathes deeply and nods. Then, she lifts the hem of her dress, revealing her thighs, her moss-green knickers, and the pale, stretched moon of her abdomen to me. Her belly button sticks out slightly, straining against the force of what's behind it.

"You're so tall, Solvig," Evie marvels. Her voice is gentle, but her eyes are blazing. "You can keep touching if you like."

I look at the backs of my hands as if they were someone else's. This time, less gingerly than before, I reach out. I feel the shiny slivers of stretch marks. The way her bump feels a little harder on one side than the other.

Evie takes off her dress. Because Evie is so relaxed, she's making this seem normal. Perhaps this is normal.

"Is that a maternity bra?" I ask, running my fingers along the fuchsia straps.

"That's right," she says. "It's a nursing bra too." She unhooks the right cup from the strap, and her breast topples out. Everything about this woman seems so full. It makes me wonder if I'm empty in comparison.

"Come on," she says, laughing, so at home in her body. She takes me by the hand and leads me to her bedroom. It's maroon, like mine. The difference is that she made her bed this morning and I didn't, and where there's an empty bottle of wine on my bedside table, on hers there's a book entitled *Architecture for Astronauts: An Activity-Based Approach.*

Evie gives me a moment to study her back—pale and strong, flecked with freckles—as she walks to the far side of the bed. Then she lies down, facing me. She sticks out her tongue. Still blue.

I look down at my loose shirt and trousers and think how thin and frail my naked body would look beside Evie's. I've been with James for so long. Our ribcages slam together when we have sex. Neither of us strives for such a skinny physique. Some people would call that lucky, but I've often wished I had fuller hips, rounder thighs. Equally, though, I've fantasised about how it might feel to rid myself of all the extraneous curves and bumps, to be as smooth and uncluttered as a Ken doll: no nipples, no genitalia, no fuss.

I undo my shirt buttons, revealing my sports bra. Letting James into my thoughts has made me feel weird. It's as though I've conjured him into the room. He's standing in the corner by the wardrobe, with a scornful, sad expression.

I take off my clothes as a dare to myself.

Wearing just my plain white underwear, I lie on the bed facing Evie. There's an ocean of duvet between us.

"Are you okay, Solvig?" she asks. "Is this okay?"

I wish I'd had more cider. Maybe I should take off my sports bra to prove how fine I am. Evie's breast is staring competitively at me. *Go on,* it's saying, through that big, dark mouth at its centre. *Show us what you've got.*

"I'd kill for your body, Solvig," says Evie, staring at my flat stomach and my protruding hip bones. "Would you mind if I touched you now?"

I shake my head and wait stoically for Evie's fingers. I focus my attention on her bump, flopped to one side because of how she's lying. I can see her heart beating in her belly, and I can see a lump too, maybe the baby's head. The lump starts to squirm.

Evie's acting like it isn't happening. Her fingertips rest on my cold skin, and I gasp.

"Solvig, why are you crying?" Evie wriggles forwards on the bed and envelops me in an embrace. "It's okay, sweetie," she says. "Shh. It'll be all right."

My body convulses as I sob. "I'm sorry . . . I thought I wanted . . . I've been looking for . . ."

"I know," says Evie, her breast squashing into mine. "I know, pumpkin."

23

I stretch out, starfish-like, and look at the ceiling. I see bits of myself reflected in the chrome lampshade. There I am: a woman in her midthirties, who has a partner and plans for a family. A woman who nearly cheated last night. I suppose I did cheat, but if I didn't sleep with Evie, and I didn't kiss her, and I didn't touch her anywhere but her stomach, would it do any good for James to know?

I sent James an apology text this morning. *Sorry I didn't call last night. Look forward to seeing you later.* Felt good to say "sorry," even if it wasn't for the thing I feel guilty about.

I also watched a YouTube video of someone crying in space. It was Chris Hadfield, former commander of the International Space Station. And he wasn't really crying. He was squirting water in his eye, to show the difference between crying on Earth and at zero gravity. A globule of clear jelly formed over his eye and then slowly spread across his face. After the demonstration, Hadfield said to the camera: "The big difference is, tears don't fall."

In the shower, I scrub my skin so hard with the loofah that it turns pink. I scrub away Evie, Center Parcs, the Mars Project. I keep scrubbing until it's just me, James, and our future baby. It hurts.

●

I'm only twenty minutes from home when I stop in a car park and rest my head on the steering wheel. I don't know how long I sit for. Time is wrapped around me like a duvet: soothing, suffocating.

When I lift my head off the wheel, I half expect to have a ticket, but there's nothing. I pay for an hour's parking and head for the centre. I walk past Lemon Quay, towards the shops on Boscawen Street. I go past tourist shops, chain stores, and boutiques, glancing in windows and dismissing everything.

Then, a white shopfront catches my eye: Mothercare. I'm meant to be looking for something for James, something that will make me feel better, but I find myself going in.

There's music playing on the speakers. A Disney tune? Something about how feeling the wind on your face can lift your heart. I run my fingers over a terry-cloth romper suit with a duckling on the front. I scrunch up a mint-green velour pinafore dress. I clutch teeny socks and mittens. I shake rattles and caress blankets.

The newborn onesies are all labelled as unisex, but there's clearly one side with a lot of pink flowers and princesses on it, and another that's full of blue tractors and dinosaurs. I like to think, as many have thought before me, that I won't gender-stereotype my daughter. Incidentally, a girl is what I feel instinctively that she's going to be. Maybe it's because I once read that divers have more female than male children. It's something to do with sperm fragility, not that this would affect me, I suppose.

I'm going to get all sorts for my daughter. Like this onesie, for instance. It's on the blue side, and it's got an orange octopus embroidered onto it. My little girl, enveloped in the many-armed embrace of a cephalopod. Symbolic, perhaps, of all the different people that are going to love her, to fold her in their arms and protect her.

"Can I help you at all?" asks a saleswoman.

"I'm having a baby," I say.

"Congratulations! When's he due?"

"It's a she. We're not sure of the exact date yet."

"Well, let me know if you need anything." She wanders off towards the prams at the back.

I hold the outfit close. This is it. The thing I am going to buy. The thing that will make me feel better.

•

James kisses me on the cheek. "Thought you'd be back ages ago."

I can hear voices in the back room. James always takes visitors in there. He thinks it's cosy. I think it smells of damp. Right now, James smells of paint stripper. "Have you been drinking?"

"Guilty as charged." James opens the front door wider and reveals a bottle of beer. I notice that he doesn't apologise for breaking our rule.

I put my rucksack down in the hall. The onesie is in there. It doesn't feel like an appropriate gift now I'm home. "You'd better get one for me too."

"Gotcha."

I follow James into the kitchen and hiss: "Who's here?"

"I threw an impromptu board game night. We're being retro and playing Scrabble." Normally, James plays geeky games like Lords of Waterdeep and Settlers of Catan. He hands me an open bottle: a wheat beer called White Noise. "How was Liverpool?"

"Work was fine." The beer tastes strong. "How come you're having a board game night tonight?"

"A few of us fancied it. Let's go through."

"But Scrabble?" I persist. "That's not your thing, is it?"

"I picked something everyone would know."

We head through to the back room and I exchange nods with Polly, Issam, and Kensa. There's one new face.

"This is Eloise," says James, taking a seat at the opposite end of the room from her. "She started renting a space at the studio last month." Eloise is petite, with a pierced septum. She's wearing a fifties-style rock 'n' roll skirt.

"Hi," she says, sipping from a can of premixed piña colada.

I sit on the carpet near James and watch him shuffle Scrabble tiles around on his rack. I can see a six-letter word (*onward*) that would bag him the triple word score, but he won't let me help. *It's right there*, I want to shout, *right there in front of you*. He plays the word *down* for eight points. Two turns later, Eloise gets the triple word score with *offal*. Forty-one points.

Later, when everyone has gone, I stand at the sink with my back to James. "She seems nice," I say, as I wash glasses. "Have you known her long?"

James takes the bottles to the front door for recycling. "A few weeks," he calls. "She was based at a studio in Newquay, but they closed down. I've been following her on Instagram for a while. She specialises in Polynesian blackwork. She's good." He comes back into the kitchen.

I empty a couple of bowls of leftover crisps into the sink.

"When's your next dive? This bin bag is overflowing."

"August." I turn to face James, forcing a smile. "That gives us two more months before I go. Two attempts."

"You're in the mood?"

"Let's go to bed," I say, with conviction.

James stares at the crisps clogging up the plughole. I can see that he's having to exercise great willpower to leave the sink as it is. "Right. Great. Let's go."

We shut Cola in the back room, which is something we've started to do when we have sex. The whining and snuffling is off-putting. *It upsets Cola to hear James like that.* That's a joke that comes into my head as we walk upstairs.

James closes the bedroom curtains. I wish he wouldn't do that. It really underlines the point that it's just the two of us that have to make this thing happen. No distractions. No input. No help.

We kiss. There's a smell that James has that I'm not keen on. I've tried to get him to wear aftershave, clean his teeth, eat more fruit, drink less coffee. None of it makes a difference. It's his natural odour. Coffee and garlic. He says that I smell of rosemary and roast chicken. Apparently, that's a turn-on.

"I've missed you," he says, lifting my jumper over my head.

"This top suits you." I take off his T-shirt.

"Wearing nothing suits you best." James pauses. "What happened?"

I'd forgotten. The graze on my shoulder, where I scrubbed it in the shower. It's round, planet-like, more revealing than a lipstick mark on a collar—it's Mars, staring James in the face. "Scraped it on a piece of equipment," I say, amazed at how easily the lie surfaces. "My own fault."

James kisses the wound, and his hot, garlicky lips make it sting.

I think about Evie. I think about Eloise.

"Home sweet home," I say, as James's ribcage slams into mine.

24

"There's such a thing as the psychogenesis of infertility," the woman in my earphones tells me. I've swapped my science podcast for an infertility one. I know we've been trying to conceive for only half a year, and in the grand scheme of things that's nothing—it's normal—but I can't bear seeing all these failed pregnancy tests. Now, from the moment I wake up to the moment my head hits the pillow, the voice drones on: *You're thirty-seven, Solvig. Past it. An infertile old mule. Time for the knackers.*

I've given up on my twenty-mile runs because too much exercise might have an adverse effect on my fertility. So, I'm going for a long walk instead. Currently, I'm power-walking past the bakery. I can smell marzipan.

"The psychogenesis of infertility," explains the woman on the podcast, whose name is Mellon, "is a theory developed in the 1950s, which says that a woman who feels ambivalent about having a baby can end up causing her own infertility. In my anecdotal experience, as a reproductive counsellor, I believe that the theory is true."

I stride quickly along the high street, dodging the push-chairs. The key to a good power walk, so they say, is to incorporate gradients into your repertoire. If you're hitting a plateau in your fitness levels, give yourself an uphill struggle.

"Be careful not to confuse ambivalence with indifference," says Mellon. "Ambivalence refers to having split feelings about something. You might simultaneously be desperate for a baby, and at the same time, or in the very next moment, feel repelled by the thought of having one. I've worked with patients who have been trying to conceive for years, who have broken down in tears about how much they want to be mothers, but they can't make peace with the idea of pregnancy. 'If I could go off into the forest for nine months,' one woman told me, 'to deal with my changing body in private, then maybe I could do it.' Many of my patients suffer from *tokophobia*, which is a pathological fear of pregnancy. It occurs even when women have no particular reason to harbour such a fear."

The word "harbour" takes me out of the podcast, and I look down an alley between two shops on my left. The harbour looks so peaceful. I wonder what sort of stuff I'm harbouring—what fears, anxieties, prejudices. Surely harbouring your negative feelings is quite sensible?

I pick up my speed now, walking so fast that people keep looking behind me to see if I'm being chased, or ahead of me, to see who I'm chasing.

There are so many reasons not to procreate. The money, the carbon footprint, the physical toll, the emotional strain. It strikes me that I haven't asked James whether he has any reservations about parenthood. I'm worried that if I open up to him, I'll shatter like Anouk's stone.

Last night, while we were having sex, I started reciting old adverts. Ones from when we were kids. "The red car and the blue car had a race . . . formulated and controlled by Laboratoires Garnier . . . turns the milk chocolatey." I think James assumed I was enjoying myself.

I'm reaching Events Square now, where the Sea Shanty Festival is being set up. Bunting and beer stalls. There's a group rehearsing in the square.

> *Goodbye, fare thee well,*
> *We're going away to leave you now,*
> *Hoorah, me boys, we're homeward bound.*

I break into a jog. The jog turns into a sprint. I run all the way up to Pendennis Point; then I look down at the water. I've spent a lot of time looking down since my trip to Sherwood Forest. Every time I look up, I feel guilty. What was it Evie said? *Every time they see the sky, I want them to think of me.*

Four more weeks and I'll be back in the diving chamber.

25

"Deano?"

My uterus is a salt marsh, a mudflat, a mangrove. It is teeming with grass shrimps and peanut worms. I feel grateful to be able to cultivate something so abundant and fruitful within my own body. I feel grateful to be able to cultivate something so abundant and fruitful within my own body. I feel grateful—

"Lad?"

I am to spend at least ten minutes a day praising my dank dwelling. I found the visualisation exercise on YouTube, and it appealed to me because I've been feeling so dried-up lately. The more I picture my uterus as a sopping wet swamp, the more right for James I feel.

"The others are calling you. Your John Skinner's ready." Dale's voice, coming from the bunk beneath me, is not conducive to a meditative state.

"On my way," I say, climbing down.

"Thought you were Bo-Peeping," says Dale. He heaves himself up to sitting. "Right. Time for work."

We're two weeks into the dive. Rich is not with us, and there have been no panic attacks, no life-or-death scenarios. It's been ten hours a day in the water, eight in the bunk, and the rest of the time for food, toilet, TV. Normally, I'd be getting lots of reading done, but I've only got Ruth Rendells and I'm not in the mood.

Kevin, Bailey, and I are on nights. Kevin is Rich's replacement. I've worked with him a few times. He once ate a whole box of doughnuts—twelve Krispy Kremes—after a morning shift. He's already halfway through his dinner when I get into the chamber.

"Took your time, lady," says Bailey.

Bailey's on the team instead of Cal, who's apparently having a wart removed. I haven't worked with Bailey before. Last night, when I came out of the loo, he asked if I'd finished "faffing around." He laughed afterwards, as if laughter were a balm that turned an insult into a joke, but I didn't laugh back.

Tai is on the dive too, working days with Eryk and Dale, but I've barely had the chance to talk to him. I've seen him on his bunk a couple of times, in between shifts. He's not reading about how to chop wood any more. Now he's reading a book called *Wills, Probate & Inheritance Tax for Dummies*.

It's 6:00 a.m. and I'm about to settle down to a scallop supper. Fortunately, time doesn't mean much in here. I think if I were outside, watching the sun rise, hearing the birds sing, I'd struggle to eat a hot dinner. In here, I can kid myself that it's six in the evening.

I sit down too fast and bash my shin on the table leg.

"That's gotta hurt," says Bailey.

Earlier on, I banged my head while getting into the bunk. I don't know what's wrong with me.

Kevin hands me my food.

Bailey passes me the chilli sauce. "Madam."

I stick the telly on. Today it's an old episode of *Star Trek: The Next Generation*. I've seen this episode before. My mum used to like *Star Trek*, so my dad tells me, and knowing that has always drawn me to it. In general, despite loving space, I'm not a sci-fi buff. I'd rather watch an action movie. The night before I left for my dive, James and I spent a good half hour surfing Netflix, trying to find something we both fancied. He wanted to watch a TED Talk on vulnerability and I wanted *Die Hard*. We compromised with a travel programme.

In this episode of *Star Trek*, the android Data is in danger of being dismantled by a scientist who wants to see his inner workings. Captain Picard must defend Data in a Starfleet court, explaining that Data is neither a slave nor a possession. Intelligent life, artificial or otherwise, must be treated with respect. Our nuts and bolts don't make us who we are—all they do is keep us from falling apart.

"She's only bloody crying," says Bailey, pointing at me.

"It's great to experience human emotions, Bailey," I say, sniffing. "You should try it sometime."

If I ever do make it to Mars, I'll need to be okay with confrontation. All sorts of issues are bound to arise. Hopefully, of course, the people who go will be polite and progressive. A microcosm of a perfect Martian society. It's the kind of thing some folk might feel sexy about: a group of men and women, living in close quarters, tasked with creating a new civilisation together. In truth, despite having joked about it with Evie at Center Parcs, I find sex in space about as appealing as sex in a compression chamber. Or sex anywhere, come to think of it.

I found myself looking at an asexual website while lying in my bunk yesterday. "Asexual people simply don't experience sexual attraction," said the website. "It's an orientation, not a choice." Apparently, you can be asexual and still be in a happy relationship. You might even experience sexual arousal; you just don't want to act on it. I wish that each time I used Google, I'd understand the universe a fraction better. Instead, it just raises new questions.

•

"Solvig," a voice whispers. "Wake up."

My eyelids flicker. "What time is it? I haven't missed my shift, have I?"

Tai is standing beside my bunk. "It's five. Can I have a quick word?"

I yawn. "Sure. What's up?"

"Not here," Tai says. "Don't want to wake the others."

I rub my eyes and climb down from my bunk. I'm wearing a tracksuit, but I still feel strangely exposed.

We head into the living chamber and sit at the table. Tai puts his palms down on the stainless steel. "My mum died," he says, "three weeks ago. I went to her funeral a couple of days before we came into saturation."

"Oh God, Tai. I'm so sorry. You could've asked for leave—"

"It's better for me to be here, to keep me occupied."

I consider telling him that my mum is dead too, but I'm not sure how it would help.

"I wanted to let you know. Since you were asking about her on the last dive." He presses the tabletop so hard that his fingernails grow pale. "How's the baby stuff going?"

"Oh, fine," I say. "Just fine."

Tai nods slowly. "I was on a woodcraft course when she took her final breaths. I should have stayed at home with her. I knew how bad she was."

I pick at a loose thread on my tracksuit bottoms. "You mustn't blame yourself, Tai." I think about how often I've told myself that if I'd been a better-behaved baby, less hard work, perhaps my mum wouldn't have needed to drink so much. I spent years torturing myself with the notion that I could have saved her.

"Life's too short," says Tai. "I feel like an idiot for going on about all that legacy stuff. All you have is now. You know?"

I look at the airlock behind Tai. Breakfast will be coming in shortly. The chefs are probably frying up my bacon rashers at this very moment.

"You're right to focus on the present," I say. "But you can keep the future on a back burner." I decide against launching into a description of the four burners theory.

"Maybe," replies Tai. "Maybe, maybe."

"Actually," I say. "Scrap that."

"Eh?"

"Fuck the future. All you have is now. You're right."

"I need to sleep," he says. "That's what I need."

26

"Where are you taking me?" asks Anouk, fiddling with the air-conditioning dial.

We're in the middle of a heatwave. I roll down the window as we wait at a red light. "That doesn't work any more," I say. "Sorry. Old banger. As for where we're going . . . you'll see."

Anouk switches on the radio. It's a local radio station, Pirate FM, and it's playing "Never Gonna Give You Up" by Rick Astley. Anouk hasn't asked how my dive went, even though I've been back for over a fortnight.

I made a decision while I was in saturation: I'm going to quit my job. I'll replace it with something that enables me to stay close to home—and close to James—all the time. That way, we can focus on our relationship and on having a baby. We can concentrate on being in love without distractions. And then, if—if—I want to do something in the future, something that puts great distance between us, like going to Mars, we'll be strong enough to weather it, because I'll have put in the hours here first.

I think Tai was right about focusing on the present. Without diving, I can be free to live the other parts of my life more fully. It's simply a case of finding a new way to be whole. And not pining for what's missing. I'm switching off some of my burners at last.

"James told me," Anouk says abruptly, as the traffic light turns green. "He told me that you're trying for a baby."

I keep looking ahead. Cornish hedgerows become unruly in the summer. "James told you we're trying?"

"He mentioned it when we went surfing."

"I'm surprised he told you."

"He has to talk to someone while you're away for a month at a time."

Since when did Anouk become bitter about my life choices? It's not like she's always taken the easy path or done what's been expected of her. And it's not like she's keeping me informed on what's going on in *her* life. I know from Facebook that Nike turned six last week, but she's barely mentioned him. She didn't invite me to the party either.

"I've been wanting to tell you, Anouk. It's just that we see each other so rarely. It's hard to get something like that into conversation."

There is a silence between us, filled only by Rick Astley.

"I'm on my period," I offer, when the song finishes.

The DJ starts talking about a syringe that's been found on Fistral Beach. We listen without speaking, and we remain like this all the way through Tresillian, Probus, and St. Mewan. When we reach St. Austell, I clear my throat. "I'm taking us to the Eden Project."

"You should've told me," Anouk says. "I've got a locals' pass. Could've brought it with me."

"Never mind. I'll buy you a ticket."

"I went at the start of the holidays."

"Well, hopefully it was good, because you're here again."

I park the car, and we head towards the site. I'm sweating horribly in this long-sleeved shirt. "So, do you know the story behind this place, then?"

"It used to be a clay pit," Anouk tells me. "Some guys came up with the idea to turn it into a garden while they were in the pub. They designed it on a napkin."

"Like the Seattle Space Needle," I say. "And the Rutan *Voyager*."

"The what?"

"The first plane to fly around the world without refuelling."

"Ah."

I buy our tickets.

There's a poster next to the desk advertising a zip wire that runs over the length of the park. It's the longest and fastest in Europe. Anouk catches me looking at it. "Is that what we're doing?"

"I thought we'd just go and look at plants," I say. "But I'm definitely up for the zip wire if you are?"

"Probably best we head for the plants," Anouk replies. "Let's be sensible." There's something about the way she says "sensible."

"It's boiling," I say, as we enter the Rainforest Biome. I look up at the glass dome above us and can't help thinking about the Subtropical Swimming Paradise at Center Parcs. I feel a sting in my gut. We shouldn't have come here. We should have gone for a glass of wine or ten.

"This is the largest indoor rainforest in the world," Anouk says.

I look around and try to practise mindfulness. Bananas, shamanic wall paintings, African totems . . . I don't know why I feel so nervous. "There's something I want to tell you, Anouk," I begin.

"There's something I want to tell you too," she says. "Can I go first?"

I nod.

"That time you babysat Nike—"

"You know I'd happily do it again. But you said you didn't want—"

"I didn't go to yoga that night."

"Oh?"

"I went night surfing."

"Night surfing?"

"Riding the waves. In the pitch black."

As we start weaving in and out of tropical plants, I say: "To be honest, Anouk, it sounds dangerous."

Anouk's eyes are shining. "It *is* dangerous. Unless you know what you're doing."

"Do you know what you're doing?"

"Not a clue."

"That's crazy."

We approach an area called "Tropical Islands," and Anouk stops by a bush marked "Croton." She twists one of the red buttons on her vest top. Her fingernail has been bitten painfully short. "I know your secret, Solvig."

I stop breathing. Has Evie somehow been in touch with her?

"It's a death sentence."

A family with two young children passes us. Anouk smiles at the parents, then scowls at me. "I'm talking about you flying off into outer space, Solvig. I take it that's what you were about to confess to me?"

"Uh, yeah. That's right."

"What are you thinking? What does James make of all this?"

More people are coming our way, so we keep walking towards a zone marked "Southeast Asia."

"How did you find out?" I ask quietly. "I haven't told anyone. Not even James."

"There are links to this thing all over the internet. Did you really think I wouldn't find out? And James? Christ's sake. Your photograph is online. And you don't look happy in it, by the way. You look like you hate yourself. You've got two hundred upvotes."

"Two hundred?"

"Yes. People are clicking a thumbs-up icon under your photograph, voting for you to die. It's ridiculous."

My cheeks are blazing. "I've got two hundred upvotes," I echo pathetically.

I wonder how many upvotes Evie has. I've been too embarrassed to risk seeing my own face on the Mars Project website, so I haven't looked. It's mortifying but thrilling to think that it's been there all this time.

Anouk stops again. "You think this is a joke? You find a one-way ticket to Mars funny? God, Solvig, I know we've grown apart lately, but this is madness. Where's your head at?"

"This means a lot to me. I know how it sounds. But it's a dream. Something I have to do."

Anouk laughs. "You have to die in space? What a superb dream."

"I probably won't die in space." I swallow. "I'll die on Mars." I look at a sign announcing that we're outside a replica of a Malaysian house known as a *kampung*. It's built from wood and straw, with a vegetable garden around it. "I want to build a home there."

"Look around you, Solvig," says Anouk. "Look at this place. Imagine living in the Amazon. And then multiply it by infinity. That's how difficult life would be on another planet. Why are you smiling?"

"Because I find this place inspiring."

"You want to build a home on Mars?" asks Anouk. "You won't have time for that. It's a suicide mission. I'll email you a list of ways you can die out there if you like. I read an article that sums it up perfectly. '10 Reasons Not to Apply for the Mars Project.'" She pauses. "You know they put your essay online, too? That thing you wrote to enter the competition? 'I want to expand man's horizons! Pain is part of the process!' Well, it's a good job you enjoy pain, girl, because it's going to be excruciating."

There's an agave plant up ahead. "*Agave americana*," it says on the sign, and beneath that: *Century plant*. There's one of these in the botanical garden in Falmouth. James pointed it out to me. He told me that each plant takes years to build up the courage to flower. James might have said "food reserves," but I prefer "courage." When it's finally ready for its reproductive act, the plant shoots up a long stalk, much taller than the original plant, taller than a man. At the top of the stalk, it grows blossoms: daring gold explosions in the sky. Shortly afterwards, it dies.

"James is going to find out," Anouk says.

I swear there's a snake coiling around my ankles. I jerk away from it, reaching out for a palm tree.

"Solvig, why are you doing that? You're acting weird. Stop it."

Anouk's voice sounds distant, as if she's speaking through a long tube. There are flecks of light, and then there's nothing.

27

10 Reasons Not to Apply for the Mars Project

1. There's not enough money in the world . . .
The team behind the Mars Project wants to raise $10 billion to put people on Mars for the rest of their lives. NASA has spent over $150 billion keeping humans alive at the International Space Station for just twenty years. Bear in mind the ISS is 250 miles away. Between Earth and Mars there are 140 *million* miles.

2. What spacecraft?
The transit vehicle that will take the astronauts to Mars is a figment of the Mars Project's imagination. It's all very well talking hypothetically about this astonishing craft, but if it doesn't exist yet, how does the Mars Project know that building it is possible? Then how does it know, without a series of highly expensive test flights, whether it would work? And how does it

operate a safe landing? Two-thirds of the forty-four missions
to Mars have failed. There's a reason space experts call Mars the
"death planet."

3. Clothes make the man . . . or break the man.
Currently, there are no specifications for the spacesuits. How
will they be pressurised? And cooled? What happens if they
tear? How reliable will they be, day in, day out, all that distance across the solar system? Mars is a long way away from
the nearest tailor.

4. Basic human needs are not so basic.
There'll be no readily available oxygen, water, or food. Sure,
the crew can take supplies, and with the right technology and
enough money, they can try to deal with these issues. They can
probably find a way to create oxygen from the carbon dioxide
that's already abundant on Mars. They can attempt to extract
water from ice deposits or hydrated minerals. And hopefully,
with research into the Martian environment, they can grow
crops to feed astronauts in future years. However, each of these
is a delicate process. It takes only one small setback, and the
results could be catastrophic. Leaks can occur. Crops can fail.
Let's face it: currently, the Mars Project doesn't even know how
basic sanitation will work. How will the crew dispose of their
own waste? This could get messy.

5. Radiation, radiation, radiation.
Space is full of particles released by the sun and stars. On Earth,
we are protected from them by the geomagnetic field and the

ozone layer. Space has neither of these things, and Mars's magnetic field is low. To travel to Mars, stay for five hundred days, and then return would likely expose astronauts to around 1 sievert of radiation. This presumes that the astronauts wouldn't get hit by a solar flare along the way, which could be fatal. The European Space Agency limits its astronauts to 1 sievert of radiation over an *entire career*. People exposed to this level of radiation have a 5 percent increased risk of dying from cancer. But the astronauts will not be living on Mars for only five hundred days. They will be living there *forever*.

6. Low gravity is, er, a grave subject.
The longest a human has spent in space is 437 days. The change in gravity during a long space mission has been seen to affect the body in the following ways: loss of bone and muscle mass, depleted calcium supplies, optical deterioration. It's possible that by the time humans reach Mars, their bodies will be so negatively affected by the gravitational changes that they won't be able to stand or see. The gravity on Mars is a third of what it is here on Earth. So even if the astronauts make it there intact, what next?

7. Life on Mars? Not for much longer.
The Outer Space Treaty of 1967 forbids the "harmful contamination" of alien environments. Yet if the crew don't have the correct procedures in place to protect any living matter that might already be on the planet, chances are they'll infect and/or kill it. And it's entirely possible that if there is something there, it could do the same to them.

8. Ashes to ashes, dust to dust.
Mars is dirty. Sandstorms last for weeks at a time. Dust can rip a spacesuit, clog a door seal, break machinery, or stop a solar panel from working. It's also high in perchlorates: toxic salts that damage the thyroid gland, weaken the immune system, and disrupt the menstrual cycle. The astronauts had better cross their fingers that these toxins don't find a way into their food or water.

9. What's the long game?
How is the civilisation on Mars meant to sustain itself? We can't keep replenishing the stock of humans on Mars from Earth. Isn't the ultimate goal that they're able to replenish themselves? Unless artificial gravity works effectively, intercourse is a massive hurdle (possibly the recent invention of the 2suit, an intimate spacesuit that accommodates two, could help with this), and besides, it's still not known whether humans are capable of conceiving in space. Even if it is possible, there's no scientific data on whether their foetuses can develop normally during the gestation period. And, if a human *can* be born in space, what will it look like? Will it make it to puberty, or die young and in agony?

10. Mad for it.
Astronauts find it hard to doze off in zero gravity, so sleep deprivation is a problem. Plus, there are the very real risks of living in confined spaces for extended periods of time. The MARS-500 project in Moscow, simulating a round trip to Mars, ended with four of the six test subjects suffering psychologically. And

that was in the space of seventeen months. Even with the most stringent testing beforehand, it's impossible to predict how people will react once they embark on a mission like this. How will astronauts cope with the idea of never returning to Earth? Leaving their families behind? Never seeing another tree, bird, or coffee shop? And if just one crew member can't handle the mission, what happens to the rest?

28

First Response: two pink lines. Lloyds Pharmacy own brand: a blue cross. Clearblue Digital: "Pregnant."

I always thought that when I eventually saw a positive test, I'd look back upon the act that had created the new life inside me with wonder. An erotic memory to savour forever.

Here's what I recall. It was the first full day back from my dive. I was nauseous and exhausted. I didn't realise that it was my fertile window because I'd switched off my app alerts, but perhaps James knew and that's why he initiated it.

"It's good to have you back," he said in my ear a little too loudly, moments after I woke. "My sourdough starter has become sluggish, but I'll nip out for some Danish pastries."

After we finished having sex, I said, "Actually, could I have a sausage roll please?"

It took me a while to put two and two together after I fainted at the Eden Project. I thought I'd started my period that day, but it must have been implantation bleeding. Ever since I took that first test, though, the symptoms have become obvious. Sore breasts. Constantly needing the loo. Headaches. I even convinced myself I had a heightened sense of smell this morning when I opened the fridge, but it could have just been that the milk was off.

Going by the date of my last period, I'm five weeks and five days pregnant. According to one website I read, that means the spinal column is in place, and the embryo may have a heartbeat. Already, so much about this baby has been predetermined. Its sex, its eye colour, its predisposition for certain diseases.

Even after I saw one positive test, I braved the first rain we've had in weeks to buy more. It was so strange, walking down the street with this enormous secret. I wondered if people could tell just by looking at me. I felt so responsible all of a sudden—so fierce—like a lioness protecting her cub. Every elbow and handbag became a potential hazard, and I put my hand over my belly, protecting the tiny spark inside me from harm.

Once I had the three positive tests lined up, I stopped testing and cried. All these months of beating myself up, telling myself I'd left it too late, eaten too much junk food, drunk too much wine, not been committed enough to the cause . . . was I finally allowed to go easy on myself?

I always felt certain that if I could just get pregnant, I'd know that this was what I'd wanted all along. The problem was that I'd had all those months to stew over the pros and cons. Yes: now that I'm pregnant, I know. This baby is for me. James is for me. The future is laid out for us, at last. It's a relief to surrender control. It's good that I didn't have to officially "quit" diving. The decision has been made for me.

Last night, I cooked James a special dinner. Newlyn hake with black olives, puy lentils, and a baked potato. All pregnancy-safe ingredients. I felt so maternal as I mashed the black olives and spread them over the pale flesh of the fish. I set the table with candles and a bunch of anemones from the garden, and then I laid out the onesie that I've been keeping balled up in my sock drawer for the last three months. There was something accusatory about the way the octopus's tentacles reached out towards me as I laid it out on the tabletop, but I heard James opening the front door before I had the chance to change my mind about it.

"Are those beluga lentils?" James said when he saw the table. Followed by: "Ooh. Candles."

Then he saw the onesie. He stroked the octopus's tentacles, and I noticed that they didn't seem accusatory with him. It was like they were beckoning him closer.

James looked up at me, tears in his eyes, and said, "Really?"

I nodded and laughed, and we hugged, and our kisses were warm seawater, and we were being baptised and reborn. It didn't matter that there'd ever been any doubt, any obstacles. We'd been rescued from our shipwreck, and we were safe on board a new vessel together.

Today, I've been on my own all day while James is at work.

I went for a run this morning, though it was more of a jog. Knowing that there's a baby inside me is a little off-putting. I know it's silly, but I worry that I'll shake it free of the womb lining or jolt it too hard and damage it. I'm focusing on tamer activities now. This afternoon, I did the laundry and took Cola for a walk around the park, although he lay down whimpering most of the time.

It's weird how life goes on in the midst of something like this. Plates still need cleaning. Carpets need hoovering. My dad had a fall at lunchtime and had to go to the doctor's. He's fine, but it was weird chatting to him and not being able to tell him my news. *You're a granddad!* I wanted to shout. *You're a granddad to a three-layered embryo, the size of a sesame seed!* I told him I hoped his bruised coccyx felt better soon.

James will be back in an hour. Not too much longer until we can daydream about parenthood together again. We're having leftovers tonight, so I don't have to do any prep for that. The only thing to do is wait.

And look at my phone.

And check for updates on the Mars Project.

And reread the article that Anouk sent me about the project's many dangers.

And accept that the dangers don't put me off. The sesame seed in my womb doesn't put me off.

Valentina Tereshkova happens to have a daughter, but she still wants a one-way ticket to Mars. Elon Musk, who has five sons, wants one too. Richard Branson has two kids, and has said he'd do it in the last ten years of his life. How he'll predict that one, I don't know, but I'll happily meet him there. Me, Tereshkova, Musk, Branson. Think of the dinner parties.

I haven't told Anouk what I made of the article. I haven't told her about being pregnant either. James has promised he won't say anything before I do. I know she'll be pleased—but she'll assume I'm giving up the astronaut stuff. I want to enjoy the pregnancy for a bit longer before Anouk starts trying to scare me again.

As for James, I'm going to tell him about Mars very soon. James is a supportive guy. I'm sure he'll understand my reasons for wanting to go. I just don't know if he'll understand my reasons for not wanting to stay.

I switch off my phone and put it down on the coffee table. I get up from the sofa and plump up the cushions. As I do this, I feel a wetness between my legs. That'll be the increased discharge I've read about. It's disgusting having to get used to things like the texture and colour of the mucus that seeps from you during pregnancy. But surprising how quickly it becomes normal. I head up to the bathroom.

As I sit on the toilet, I look down at my knickers. But I don't see any mucus. I see a bright red smudge. In the centre of the smudge is a clot. Looks like a slice of liver. It's the size of a sesame seed.

I grab a pregnancy test from the shelf behind me and follow the instructions on the back of the box. I rest it on the radiator and look at my watch.

I bought these knickers from Marks & Spencer. They're white with green diamonds on them. They came in a multipack. I had no inkling, when I bought them, that they'd play such a pivotal role in my life. I take them off and look at the clot more closely. It has no distinguishable features. It smells of me. I smell of it.

It's early, but I can't hold out any longer. I look at the test.

A faint second line is appearing.

My jaw unclenches. I exhale. Thank God for that.

This is more implantation bleeding.

I wipe myself with the toilet roll. There's more blood. I can feel it trickling out of me now, and I feel a twinge in my cervix as it comes out.

The test has had three minutes. The faint second line hasn't grown any darker. It's a ghost. I drop it in the bin.

I feel another spasm, and I pass more blood. I wipe it away and get off the toilet, but I don't know what to do with my knickers. I don't want to put them back on, but I don't want to leave the clot alone. So I hold on to them. But I don't touch the baby in case I damage it—it'd be like touching a butterfly wing.

My whole world is in the palm of my hands. My whole world is a glob of blood, a slice of liver, a butterfly wing. Nothing else matters.

I curl up on the floor, pressing my cheek against the cold vinyl. Sliver by sliver, I bleed and fall apart.

"Oh no, Solvig."

Time has passed and James is looking down at me.

29

Tonight's full moon means I don't have to switch on any lights. I can even see the floorboards, and I know exactly where to step so that I don't make any creaks.

I go into the spare room and walk over to the window. I wish I could open it and dive straight into the sea. I wonder what creatures are out there now, swimming in the moonlight. The sea serpent Morgawr, perhaps? Another Cornish legend.

Sometimes at this time of year we get the odd bluefire jellyfish washed up on the shore. James was so excited when we found one last summer. Normally they live in colder waters. They live for a year and will sting you even when they're dead. I've never been stung by one, but I did tread on a sea urchin once. I was on holiday with my dad in Lanzarote. A local barman had to pull the spines out of the sole of my foot with tweezers, and then he shaved off the pedicellariae with a razor. I don't know what the pedicellariae were, exactly. Dad and I couldn't understand the barman very well. It was something to do with the sea urchin's mouth, or possibly anus. Afterwards, I threw up, and vowed never to go near the sea again. A couple of days afterwards, though, my foot felt better, and I was back on the beach, building sandcastles.

The miscarriage happened ten days ago. I went to the doctor the morning after it happened. The appointment was delayed, so I had to sit in the waiting room with James for over an hour, watching two identical twin girls in the play area building a tower with green bricks, then demolishing it, then building it, then demolishing it. I almost screamed at the mother to stop them from repeating this endless cycle, but James put his hand on my arm and told me he'd take me for lunch afterwards. We'd go and eat some brie or salami or smoked salmon.

"I think I've had a miscarriage," I told the doctor while James sat in the waiting room.

"It doesn't say on your notes that you were pregnant," she replied.

"I hadn't got around to telling you. But I was. And I don't think I am any more." I got out my phone and showed her a photo of the clot.

The doctor barely looked at the photograph. "Let's do a blood test to confirm either way, shall we?" She took an empty vial and stuck a needle in my arm. My blood came out almost black. Not like the bright red stuff I'd seen the day before.

"You can phone for the results tomorrow," the doctor said. "In the meantime, I wouldn't be too hopeful. This is your first pregnancy, yes?"

I burst into tears, and I was instantly angry with myself for crying in the presence of someone so heartless. "We've been trying since January," I said. "I think there's something wrong."

The doctor handed me a tissue. "You're thirty-seven," she said, "which probably isn't helping matters. It's only going to get tougher with each passing month. But it's still too early to think about treatment. We'll see what the results of this test say, all right? If it's bad news, you'll need to keep trying for a full twelve months before we can refer you for tests."

"What if I'd lied and told you we'd been trying since last October? Would you have referred me then?" I asked.

The doctor typed something on my notes but didn't answer.

"Is it my fault? Is it because I'm a saturation diver? Is my body a hostile environment?"

The doctor stopped typing and looked at me over her glasses. "It's just one of those things."

I knew that the test results would come back negative. The doctor said my hCG level was four mIU per millilitre. Anything under five is considered zero. There's no official evidence that I was ever pregnant.

How do you grieve something that never existed?

Or what if it did exist, but only barely? It scraped the edge of happening and then veered off course.

The cluster of cells inside me obviously managed to implant itself into the lining of my womb, or I wouldn't have seen all those tests read positive. But what happened next? Did the cells fall out again? Was there a chromosomal abnormality, which meant that if they *had* grown to be the size of a baby—if my body hadn't disrupted that chain of events—perhaps the cells wouldn't have grown into a baby at all, but just one oversized spleen, or half an eyeball, or an unidentifiable lump of human meat?

There was something wrong with my baby, if I'm even allowed to call a failed embryo a baby, and I'll never know what it was. I'll never know if it was a girl or a boy, or if it could have rolled its tongue, or if it would have had a Darwin's tubercle on its ear.

I've been in bed for most of this week, staring at the ceiling. I've given the baby a name: Lucy. I felt that she was a *she* while she was inside me, so that's what I'm going to believe. Lucy is the name scientists gave to a three-million-year-old skeleton they found in Ethiopia. Lucy is one of our earliest ancestors, and, according to the Beatles song she was named after, she is also in the sky with diamonds.

I go to the shelves opposite the window and look at the boxes of equipment. I fetch the things I'm going to need: a tattoo gun, ink, machine tips, power source, needles, wet wipes, latex gloves. I lay them out on the desk by the wall and sit down.

The needles are all so big. Not like sewing needles. These ones must be fifteen centimetres long. I try to find a tip and needle that look like they fit together. It's hard to tell without unwrapping them, so I put on a pair of gloves and take some out. Finally, I find a pair that match. This needle is one of the thicker ones, which isn't ideal. In fact, it's made up of about fifteen needles and looks like a miniature comb. Never mind. As long as it's pointy.

I push the tip into the tattoo gun, then insert the needle carefully, knowing how easily these things can break. I secure the needle with a rubber band, as I've seen James do, and press the trigger to test it. The end of the needle pops out. When I release the trigger, it pops back in again. That's good. This is going to work.

I attach the gun to the power source and pedal; then I pour out some black ink into a plastic container and dip in the needle. I rest my forearm on the desk, wrist up.

I've heard some people describe tattoos as pleasurable, and I've heard others describe them as torture. James talks of the *pain curve*. He says the first couple of minutes of getting a tattoo are intense, as your body is getting used to what's happening. But soon, you start to make endorphins, and they give you an hour or two of natural pain relief. During this stage, James says, some people find the experience of getting a tattoo quite enjoyable. And then, if you're getting a bigger piece done, your body starts running low on happy chemicals. When that happens, you'll likely need regular breaks, and you'll feel relieved every time the gun breaks contact with your skin. Even the toughest guys can be shrieking in agony after a five-hour-long rib piece.

I've never had a tattoo, but I have been in pain before. I had my wisdom teeth removed a few years ago, and the anaesthetic didn't work properly on one side. That was bad. I've burned myself welding a couple of times too. Nothing horrific, but enough to cause the skin to blister.

I push my foot down on the pedal. The buzz of the machine startles me. I take a deep breath. Best way to do this, I figure, is quickly. Don't overthink it. I press the needle into my skin.

Blood pools on my wrist. The needle must have gone too deep. I get a wet wipe and mop it up. I'm left with a thick, reddish-black smudge. It doesn't look much like an *L*, but perhaps it will when it dries.

I hurry out a *U* and a *C*. This time there's just a trail of black dots—I haven't gone deep enough. I'll have to redo it in a minute. I press harder for the *Y*.

"Solvig, what's going on?" James is standing in the door-way, in his boxers. He hasn't got his prosthesis on, and he's holding the door frame for support. "Put down the gun. Please."

I want to take my foot off the pedal, but I've turned to stone.

"Stop it, love."

"It hurts so much," I say.

When I release the pedal, the machine stops buzzing, but now I can hear the whooshing inside me.

James hops over to my chair and puts on some latex gloves, then sets about wiping up the mess I've made.

"What's that?" I ask, as he applies a layer of ointment.

"Baby rash cream," he says. "It'll protect the wound."

I can smell his body. It's the smell I know well, but I feel as though I'm smelling it for the first time. I always thought it was coffee and garlic. Now it's hazelnut, cider apple, moss. It's the smell of the man who loves me, who is wrapping cling film around my wrist, taking care of me.

"Sorry," I say, as James holds me.

"It's okay." James strokes my hair. "Let's go back to bed."

We lie between the sheets, and I mentally trace the name "Lucy" on the ceiling, wondering when the pain will end. A long time goes by, maybe hours.

"I think I'll cancel my appointments today," says James, fi-nally breaking the silence.

In the garden, the siskins sing their songs—*tilu, tilu, tilu*—and the weak October sunshine begins nudging its rays through the grey curtains.

I squeeze James's hand. "I've missed you," I tell him.

"I've missed you too."

I nuzzle his neck, and I look, really look, at him. "Make love to me," I whisper.

James takes me in his arms, and slowly, over the course of the next hour, he kisses me from head to toe. He fulfils my request, more literally than ever before.

When we are finished, I roll onto my side, looking at the black smudge beneath the cling film on my wrist. It looks like an oil spillage. I can just about make out the letters *L* and *Y*. "Lie," I say quietly.

"Pardon?" James kisses me behind the ear.

"I never want to lie to you again."

"That's good. I don't want to lie to you either."

"I've got a secret."

The sun shines more brightly now. With my back to James, I look at the white wall opposite me, and I talk about Evie. I don't mention Center Parcs or Mars. I simply talk about a woman I met while I was away from home. I explain that although nothing happened, there was a space between us. A space that was significant.

PART THREE

30

"He's been gone for nearly three weeks. Staying with his parents in Penzance. He won't answer my calls."

"That sounds stressful," says the woman with a Northern Irish accent, who identified herself as Rachel at the start of our phone conversation.

"It is." I'm out of breath, navigating my way over spiky grey tufts of marram grass. I'm walking over sand dunes, heading away from the main beach, towards the cliffs at Kelsey Head.

"What was it that made James feel he wanted some time away?" Rachel asks.

She probably thinks I'm being abused. Or I'm addicted to drugs. Or I'm depressed. I'm not depressed.

TripAdvisor says that at low tide, you can see an Argentinian shipwreck here. The tide is lowish now, but it's rising, and I can't see anything except water.

"James went away because of something I told him. It was something that happened back in June. Me and another woman. All we did was lie together."

"What were your feelings towards her?"

I scramble over a large rock, careful not to slip on the seaweed. A few years ago, a scourge of toxic turquoise algae appeared on Porth Beach. It bloomed after a long, hot summer, killing the fish and irritating people's eyes and skin.

"I was intrigued," I say eventually. "And jealous. I wanted to be inside her. Not sexually. I mean, I wanted to feel what it was like to *be* her. Is that weird?"

Finally, I come to a long vertical slit in the rocks. The entrance to Holywell Cave.

"Did you speak to James about these feelings?"

"No, of course not." I step inside the slit. "He wouldn't understand. I barely understand."

Inside the cave, I can make out limestone formations, like poured concrete. Higher up, there's another, smaller cave entrance. Fresh water is trickling out of it.

The rocky steps leading up there look slippery, but I reckon I can climb them if I take it slow. I'm going to have to put the phone down, though, so I wait where I am for now.

"What did James say when you told him about the woman?"

I think back to that day. The sun through the curtains. The sting of the tattoo. The question James asked several times, which I did not manage to answer for him: *Why?*

"He told me that he knows things have been difficult. He's seen me struggling since the start of the year, since he suggested we try for a baby. If he's honest, he saw me struggling before that too. He thought trying for a baby would make things better. He made a mistake. He shouldn't have asked. He feels bad."

"And the woman? What did he say about her?"

"He told me that a relationship is a collage. New layers bury old ones. There are dark bits, bright bits, rough bits, smooth bits. He told me that our glue pot is empty. There's nothing left to stick the pieces together. The glue is trust. The trust is gone." That's not all James said. He also said: "Fuck you, Solvig."

"Do you think that the trust can be rebuilt?"

I look down at my hiking boots. I'm standing in a puddle. You're not meant to come here when the tide is rising. I shouldn't hang around. I say: "How are you meant to know what you want?"

"You're not sure that the trust is worth getting back?"

I look at my wrist. The scab looks like a grey cloud. I'm hoping that when it falls off there'll be something glorious underneath, but I know that there won't be. It's just an illegible scrawl. In places where I've pushed too deep, I've got subcutaneous ink seepage. *Blowout*, James called it. The ink has blurred like a permanent bruise. At least the infection has subsided. Turns out I didn't clean the area properly before I started. James made sure to tell me about wound aftercare before he left for Penzance. That's the kind of person he is.

"I was pregnant," I tell Rachel. "For five weeks and five days. Or, technically, if you go from conception, less than a fortnight. We were trying for nine months. I didn't know if it was what I wanted, but then it happened, and I was excited. And then it ended, and I was sad."

"I'm very sorry to hear that, Solvig."

I take a quick look at the time. I need to hurry up. "That woman—the one I lay down with—was pregnant. I felt like I wanted to find her sexy, but I didn't. When I was pregnant,

James said I was amazing, gorgeous . . . all these things I didn't feel."

"I wonder if there's a way that you can—"

"It's like the Venus of Willendorf debate."

"The what, sorry?"

"There's this Palaeolithic figurine, made of limestone," I say, running my fingers along the walls of the cave. "James and I watched a TED Talk on it. The archaeologists who found her assumed she was an erotic sculpture because of her voluptuous figure, but later, other people thought maybe she wasn't erotic at all—that she was a symbol of fertility. Her round belly was carrying a child. Most people view the figurine as one or the other: erotic or fertile."

"You mean, rather than seeing it as both at the same time?"

"Exactly. The mother or the lover." After I put the octopus onesie on the table, James got us to watch the entirety of TED's pregnancy series.

"Is that how you feel, Solvig? That you can't be both?"

"Is it bad that I don't feel drawn towards either? I'd rather go to Mars." Saying it outright feels freeing. "Yes. I want to go to Mars."

Obviously, Rachel doesn't get the significance of this. "How are you feeling now?"

"I suppose I'm wondering something. If it's okay for me to not know what I want, then what happens when I need to make a decision?"

"Well, you need to—"

My reception cuts out.

I put my phone in my pocket. Never mind.

I look up at the hole in the rocks above me, and then I head towards it. I crouch to enter the cave.

Inside, I perch on a slab, and I switch on the light on my phone. Everything is pink and glistening.

The water in this cave is said to be holy. This has been a pilgrimage site for hundreds of years, helping ease sickness and grief. I dip my hand into a shallow pool and feel a tingle run up my arm, straight to my heart.

"Mum," I whisper. "I miss you."

My voice echoes around the chamber.

Mum's ashes ended up in the sea. Dad tipped them off the pier at Weston-super-Mare. He left me at home with my aunt Marie. I don't remember that day, but I do remember searching for my mum in rock pools while I was on holiday in South Wales.

I wonder when my next dive will be. Obviously, I haven't quit diving yet—not now that everything's so uncertain. If James is going to leave me, what's the point? But I'm not missing it as I normally do.

Soon, the water will rise so much that going back won't be an option.

I climb down the steps and emerge into the afternoon sunlight, flooded with unexpected relief.

As I retrace my steps back towards the main beach, my phone vibrates. Is Rachel calling to check I haven't killed myself? Is James ready to talk? No. It's a London number.

"Miss Dean," says an unfamiliar male voice. "This is Pim Jansen. I'm a recruiting assistant at the Mars Project. I'm not sure if you realise this, but your online entry has amassed over one thousand votes. In addition to this, you impressed the moderator at the conference you attended."

"I did?"

"We love your CV, Miss Dean. Your diving experience is of particular interest. I'm delighted to inform you that we have selected you for an interview, which will take place at the end of the month in Washington, DC."

"An interview? In Washington? I thought you were based in the Netherlands?"

"The fantastic news is that we've recently entered into a partnership with a popular American soda company. This incredible dream of ours is very quickly becoming a reality!" The stranger informs me that he'll send an email confirming my flight details. He wishes me good luck.

Good luck.

I'll need it, although I'm not sure which direction to channel it in.

I know it's so unlikely, and it's probably just a miscarriage thing, but my period is late again.

31

I'm at the Rumbling Tum. It's an alleyway café between the high street and the harbour. Normally, if James were here, we'd go to one of the hipster hangouts like Beerwolf: a bookshop-cum-bar with retro arcade machines in the corner and creepy dolls hanging from the rafters. Or Espressini for a strong AeroPress coffee, brewed by our friend Issam.

But I can't risk seeing anyone I know. I expect James has told people what's been going on between us.

I'm not sure whether James has spoken to Anouk yet. I'm guessing not, because she hasn't been in touch. Which means she doesn't know about the pregnancy or the miscarriage or Evie. I think there's a limit to how much you can hide from your best friend. If you keep too many secrets, you're not really friends any more, are you?

James came home last night and packed another bag. He took some nature encyclopaedias, which he uses for reference at work, plus some Kilner jars, because he says fermenting vegetables is his new raison d'être. He's staying between his parents' house and Eloise's flat now. When he told me about Eloise, I felt a sudden, jubilant sense of vindication.

"I knew you were sleeping with her," I said.

"Eloise is going out with Kensa," James replied. "She's a friend. You're the one who cheated, Solvig."

I bite into my sausage and egg roll, feeling the yolk dribble down my chin. I eat hungrily, even though I feel sick. Really sick. Worryingly sick. The greasy food makes me feel better, if only briefly.

It's been six weeks since the miscarriage, and my period still hasn't come. I can't think about it right now. I flick through the *Daily Mail* lying on the table, left behind by the last customer. Same old stories: election fraud, Russian spies, gun control, Brexit. I turn the page, and a headline catches my eye.

FIRST HUMANS ON MARS WILL DIE
WITHIN THREE MONTHS
The controversial Mars Project may soon have the fund-
ing to send humans to the red planet, but according to
boffins at the Massachusetts Institute of Technology
(MIT), inhabitants would start dying after just 68 days.

As I finish my roll, I drop a dollop of ketchup onto the article, smearing it with red. I'm about to close the paper, to hide the mess I've made, but I'm distracted by another story.

MOTHER OF THREE SAYS FINAL
GOODBYES TO HER CHILDREN

31-year-old Sandra from Merseyside is suffering from
a rare form of cancer, and has decided to travel to Swit-
zerland to end her life with help from the not-for-profit
assisted suicide organisation that has been running since
1998. There have been only 90 or so recorded cases of
leiomyosarcoma of bone since its discovery in 1965. It is
a particularly aggressive illness, and the survival rate is
estimated to be around two years.

"The pain is already unbearable," said the mother of
three, who will be ending her life with assisted suicide
next week. "As the cancer grows, my bones will start to
fracture, and I'll have trouble breathing."

Five months ago, Sandra underwent surgery for her
condition, but it was unsuccessful. She has decided not
to put herself or her family through the heartache of
undergoing chemotherapy, which leiomyosarcoma is
generally resistant to in any case. Her eldest child, Leila,
aged 11, said, "Mummy is very brave. I will miss her."

How could Sandra do that? Not even try? How could she
voluntarily kill herself without trying *every single other option* first? Her children might think she's brave now, but I bet
they'll resent her later.

If my mum had been in that situation, she'd have tried everything to stay alive. Acupuncture, crystals, religion, the lot.

Saying that, my mum did have options. She didn't have to
go out to a work party that evening. She didn't have to leave
the nightclub at 2:00 a.m. without her colleagues. She could
have got a taxi home, instead of walking. She could have not

been drunk. She could have looked where she was going. She could have avoided the subdural haematoma which killed her almost instantly. She abandoned us. Just as Sandra is doing with her kids.

I take my phone out of my pocket and call my dad.

"Sol. How goes it, kiddo?"

I walk out of the café towards the water. "Dad, can I come and stay at yours for a bit?"

"Sorry, love. Can you speak up a bit?"

"Can I stay with you, Dad?"

"Oh, listen. Normally, I'd say yeah, right? But, thing is, Reveka's on strike. She's refusing to make the bed or cook. Bit of a bomb site up here. How abouts I come and stay at yours for a few days? Been feeling a bit under the weather lately, anyway. Sea air'd do me good, I reckon. Be nice to see your neck of the woods again."

"Just you, then? No Reveka?"

"Just me, pup. That okay?"

I cry and say yes. Yes, please. Come as soon as you can.

32

"Got my disability money," says Dad, edging down the stairs. "How about we go down the pub? We could take Cola. What do you say, Hokey Cokey?"

Cola is asleep. We already went for a walk today.

My dad reaches the bottom step and pokes the dog with his foot. "Come on, boy. Can't get past you when you're lying there, can I, you big lug?"

I've often wondered why my dad won't get a dog. It'd do him good to have a companion other than one of his carers. One that he could look after, instead of vice versa.

"How's your back, Dad?" I ask, sliding Cola along the carpet to make room for my dad's feet.

"Oh, you know," he says. "Totally annihilated."

We go into the kitchen, and I grab the dirty cups and plates off the counter and put them in the sink.

"Come on then, Sol. What do you say? It'll be dinnertime soon if we don't get a wriggle on. Couple of swifties?"

"Fine," I relent, "but we'll eat out. I can't be bothered to cook when we get back."

"Right you are," says my dad, rubbing his hands together. "Fish and chips it is."

I grab my jacket and scarf, and we leave the house. It's surprisingly balmy for a November evening, but the weather can change rapidly here. We make our way slowly down the hill towards town.

"This is the life, isn't it, eh?" wheezes Dad. "Fresh air. Seagulls. Does you good being in a place like this. No wonder you look so healthy, kid."

I bite my lip and point out some local landmarks: art gallery, maritime museum, plaque commemorating a visit by Charles Darwin.

"Very nice," Dad says. "Very nice indeed. Hang on a mo. The pharmacy is still open. I'll just nip in for my meds."

We go into the pharmacy, and an old-fashioned bell rings above the door. Dad makes a beeline for the dispensary at the back of the shop. He certainly doesn't fake his pain, but I can't help noticing that he's hobbling more than usual now that he's surrounded by medication. He takes a slip of green paper out of his pocket and talks to the pharmacist.

I stay by the door, looking at the boxes and bottles on the shelves beside me. I wonder how you'd go about organising the products in a place like this. Alphabetical order? Heads, shoulders, knees, and toes? By the looks of it, they've squeezed stuff in wherever it fits. For example, beside a packet of suppositories, there's a First Response pregnancy test.

I steal a look at my dad. He's making a fuss about having to sign the back of the prescription, as if he hasn't had to do that a million times before. The pharmacist is patiently pointing out the line he needs to put his signature on, perhaps wondering if the years spent at university have all been a bit of an anticlimax.

As nonchalantly as possible, I pick up the pregnancy test and walk over to the counter at the front of the shop. A ginger-haired girl, sixteen at the most, takes the box and scans the barcode. "Chocolate for a pound?"

"No thanks," I reply, wondering if she offers this to everyone or if I'm getting special treatment because I might be pregnant. I look over at my dad, then take a lipsalve from a plastic jar and give that to the girl too. She rings it through the till, and I hand over the cash. I push the test deep into my coat pocket and go outside.

Most of the shops are closed now. The lights of KFC look oddly romantic in the early evening. Families huddle around tables at the windows, exchanging stories over their red buckets of fried chicken.

My dad comes out of the pharmacy waving a paper bag. "The good stuff."

I make a big show of putting on the lipsalve I bought. "Mmm, strawberry," I say. "Couldn't resist."

We walk on until we reach the 'Front. I don't come here often, as it can get a bit rowdy. There's always something happening: funk and soul night, quiz night, Breton folk music night. Not my kind of thing. But it's on the harbour, and it serves decent beers.

Last time my dad came down to Falmouth, I took him to the specialist craft ale bar, Hand. He had a 7 percent saison beer called The Emptiness Is Eternal, and he told the barman it tasted like piss. Didn't stop him from ordering two more and then chanting football anthems so loudly James and I had to take him home.

The 'Front bar is much more traditional: Cornish flag bunting and pints of Betty Stogs on tap. It has a low, vaulted ceiling, giving it the air of a smugglers' inn. It's tucked away beneath Trago Mills, a discount department store with a UKIP billboard nailed to the side of it. I'm trying to block out the fact that on the way here, my dad looked up at the billboard and said: "Not long now till we get our country back, eh?"

"Well," Dad says, settling into his chair with a pint. "This is nice."

I've ordered myself a red wine. After all, I don't know for sure that I'm pregnant. Drink till it's pink, so they say.

"Dad?" I ask. "What was it like? You know, after Mum died? Did you ever feel angry with her?"

"Angry, pup?" He opens the paper bag he got at the pharmacy and takes a blue tablet out of the box inside. I'm not sure he should be mixing pain medication and alcohol, but if I say anything, he'll tell me I'm nagging. "Wasn't her fault she died. Or do you mean angry at her for something else?"

I fiddle with the stem of my wine glass. "If she hadn't gone out drinking . . ."

"Accidents happen, Sol. You know that, in your line of work. So do I, that's for sure." He opens a packet of pork scratchings.

"But she didn't die doing something worthwhile." I swallow a large mouthful of wine. "She tripped over a post."

Dad chews thoughtfully on a piece of pork. "Your mum made mistakes, like all of us," he says. Then, his voice cracks: "She'd be so proud of you now."

"I don't know. Mum was a genius. I mean, you're really talented too, Dad, but—"

Dad bursts into laughter. "Your mum was a bright woman, yes. But not as clever as you, chuck."

I shake my head. "But Mum was always working on something. Like that notepad you said she kept by her bed, where she'd write down ideas in the dead of night. I can go for months without working."

Dad takes a long draught of his pint. It leaves a moustache of foam on his upper lip. "Your mum was a workaholic," he says, wiping his mouth. "She was an insomniac too. When she woke up in the wee hours, it wasn't quadratic equations she was scribbling down. It was shopping lists, or reminders to record *Mastermind* off the telly. Sometimes she'd write down targets, things she wanted to achieve. She could never just relax and enjoy the moment, your mum. Always worrying about what was to come. The only way she could chill out was with a drink. But she'd always take it too far. Especially after she had you."

"I . . . was too much for her?"

"She loved you to bits. She really did. Having a baby was overwhelming for her, though. She'd start playing with you or feeding you or whatever, and she'd get so frustrated. You'd spend ten minutes together, and then she'd be calling to me out in the studio, begging for me to take over. I didn't mind. Quite liked it. Cuddling a baby instead of working."

My face feels tingly. I feel so disgusted by my dad so frequently. Not to mention confused about how someone like my mother could have married him. I've often felt angry with Mum because she was the one to die and not my dad. Maybe I've been angry with my dad for not dying.

"I'll be back in a minute," I say, heading for the toilets, still wearing my coat. I go into a cubicle and take the test out of my pocket.

First Response. If the test is positive, I honestly can't predict what my first response will be.

I've done this so many times now. I know exactly what angle to place the stick at, how many seconds to keep it in my urine stream, how long to wait afterwards. I replace the cap and lay the test across my thighs.

I'm not ready to do this again.

I'm not ready for so many reasons.

I look at the graffiti on the cubicle walls: "Trans rights NOW." "Do what makes you happy!" "This is the closest we will ever be."

Whatever the result is, I don't want to feel emotionally connected to it. You can't fall in love with a line, or grieve over the lack of one. I want to be able to look at the test, acknowledge whether there's one band or two, throw it in the bin, and then figure out what to do next. It's just a series of processes. Simple as that.

I close my eyes and exhale slowly. "Do what makes you happy!"

I open my eyes.

Two lines.

The test line is darker than the control line. It's much, much darker than it was last time around. With Lucy.

"This is the closest we will ever be."

I put the test in my pocket, flush, and head back into the pub.

Dad has lined up three coasters along the edge of the table. He flips and catches them one by one.

There's Granddad, up to his old tricks, I think.

"Another pint, Dad?" I ask.

Dad sighs, as if he has the weight of the world on his shoulders. "Yeah, why not?"

I could answer this question. I could answer it at length. I don't.

I get us some drinks and sit down. I've still got half my wine left. Fuck it. I'm going to finish it before moving on to the soft drink.

"What you got there?" Dad looks at my lemonade.

"G and T. Fancied something refreshing."

Dad nods and sips his pint.

I feel weird drinking my wine. A pregnant woman on the sauce. I know that, technically, it's not like pregnant women are banned from booze, but it does feel transgressive. Not in a good way. How much can it affect a baby at this stage, though? It's not like the baby has taste buds yet. It's not like the baby has a liver or a brain. Maybe it does. How many weeks am I now? I'm further along than I was with Lucy.

I put down my glass and glance at my pocket, making sure the test isn't poking out. I can feel its presence as though it were red hot. I want to scream or be sick. I grip the table like it's a cliff edge. "So, how are things with Reveka?" I ask.

Dad wrinkles his nose. "Reveka? Says I don't show enough interest in her sprog. Wants me to go to this music recital he's doing. Plays the bassoon, apparently."

I don't remember my dad coming to any of my choir performances when I was younger. I only really went to choir practise because Chris Fox was an alto. I'd have hated my dad to have seen me gawping at Chris as I sang cantatas. Or at least, that's what I told myself, because Dad never came.

My jealousy must be written on my face, because Dad says: "Couldn't stand all that stuff when you were little. Recitals and plays and whatnot. Sitting there on me tod, while all the other mums and dads played happy families."

"I thought you didn't come because of the 'pomp and ceremony.'"

Dad throws a pork scratching into his mouth. "Yeah, that too." He chews for a long time before swallowing, and then says: "You know, I got really down in the dumps last year. Remember when I said I couldn't come to yours at Christmas? Told you I had the flu? I went to Wetherspoon's for a turkey pie. Just me and my shadow. Didn't feel like company. But then I met Reveka. She made me feel better. I haven't treated her right. I never get it right."

That's not true, I want to say. *It's me that keeps messing up.*

I listen to Dad as he discusses what went wrong with all his old carers, and why Reveka is different. I listen as he talks about women and how complicated they are for two more rounds.

After draining the dregs of his fourth pint, he looks at me, hazy-eyed, and says: "Not thirsty tonight, kid? Ah well. Fancy a moon walk?"

"Moon walk?"

"Yeah, you know. A night-time stroll. Clear away the cobwebs."

"Oh, right. Sure, Dad." My voice is softer and more child-like than it was earlier. "As long as we can get chips."

My dad gets up unsteadily and ruffles my hair. "Blimey, Sol, when did you last wash this mop?"

We head out of the pub. The sky is layered with dusky pinks. The tiniest slice of moon is showing. It's a waning crescent. In a couple more days, it will surrender into oblivion.

Dad whistles. "Impressive, innit?"

"Always," I say, looking up.

"Red sky at night, I guess."

We go around the corner and get ourselves chips in poly-styrene cones, then start walking along the harbour.

"You probably don't remember this," says Dad, skewering several chips at once with his wooden fork. "But there was this one holiday we went on. Me and you and your mum. Your mum passed away that winter, but this was the summertime. You must have been two. Your mum, she let you have a battered sausage. It was at the beach, in Skegness. You picked up the sausage like this, with your fingers in pincers, and after licking it for a bit, you dropped it in the sand. You were so upset that—"

Dad does that awkward dance with someone for a few moments, where you're trying to pass each other, but you keep looking like you're about to butt heads. Finally, they pick different directions and walk on.

"People everywhere tonight," he says.

There's a group of women heading towards us, all wearing purple T-shirts saying "Night-Time Memory Walk" on the front. They've got purple wigs on, too, plus glow-stick necklaces and bracelets.

"Bet they're cold," says Dad.

"What happened after I dropped the sausage?"

"You buried it. Dug a grave in the sand so the seagulls couldn't have it. Made me and your mum say a few words."

I smile. "What did you say? Can you remember?"

"Oh, something like, 'Goodbye sausage, you were loved. May you rest in peace. Mushy peace.'"

"Very funny."

"It was sweet, though, seeing how much you cared. We asked if you wanted another and you burst into tears." He puts a greasy hand around my shoulder and kisses me on the forehead with salty lips. "Love you, pup."

We zigzag through the cobbled streets, towards home. There's a group of women in purple T-shirts lighting candles and laying them down around a stone fountain. Some of them are clasping hot drinks. One or two of them are laughing. Many of the candles have photographs next to them.

"Dad?" I say, reaching into the bottom of my chip cone and collecting the crispy bits.

"Yes, Sol?"

"Thanks for looking after me."

Dad squeezes my hand. He doesn't say anything else all the way back home. When we get in, I see how tired he looks.

"I'd better hit the hay," he says. He looks so much smaller than me these days. When did I overtake him?

I give him a glass of water and make him a hot-water bottle, and then I sit at the kitchen table. I listen to the clock ticking for a while. Reminds me that I've got my Mars interview coming up. Reminds me of everything.

I creep upstairs; then I sit on my bed and take a folder out of the bottom drawer of my bedside table. This is the folder that Dad gave me: Mum's stuff.

I pull out the top few sheets of paper and look again at the computer game my mum was designing. "Blue hall." "Weapons deck." "Outskirts of village." "Broken cage." "Metal floor." Her handwriting really is manic.

I look again at the letters she wrote beside the lines connecting boxes: *P, S, A, F, U, D. Port and starboard*, I think suddenly. *Aft and fore*. I know my nautical terms. But *U* and *D*? What could they be? Up and down?

I switch on my phone and go to Safari. In the search box, I type in some of the phrases on the page. The first result that comes up is entitled "Game Solution: Starcross." The second is a Wikipedia entry. I select that.

It tells me that *Starcross* was a computer game released in 1982. It's set in the future, and the player's character is a lone space traveller on the lookout for treasure in black holes. One day, he finds a mysterious spacecraft and climbs on board looking for answers . . .

I know that it shouldn't matter that Mum didn't design this game. I know it's okay that these are only notes she made for a game that she was playing. A game designed by someone else.

It's just: I really did think she was a genius. A pioneer. I thought she had grand plans. But the mother I've been dreaming about is a mythical creature. My actual mother, the mother I can see here, the mother my dad told me about tonight—she was as confused and scared as I am.

I put the paper back into the folder and hug my knees. I bite my right leg through my jeans. This is a position I've adopted ever since I was a girl. I could sit like this for an hour at a time back then. Now it's not so comfortable.

"Argh," I say quietly, to my knee. "Argh."

I sit up straight again and look out of the window at the waning crescent. There's an urban legend that all twelve men who walked on the moon went mad upon their return to Earth.

At least they were able to return.

33

James has agreed to meet me for a walk along the promenade. *A promenade in Penzance.* The reality is not as splendid as it sounds. B&Bs, a petrol station, and an enormous Lidl don't do the seafront any favours. Nor do the Christmas decorations hanging over the roads. Pale Santas and ghostly wreaths loom unlit in the November sky.

For a moment, I don't recognise him as he approaches. His hair is scraped back into a bun. He's got a neck tattoo—a neck tattoo! Most remarkable of all, he's wearing glasses. They're thin and round, in the "John Lennon" style. As far as I'm aware, James has twenty-twenty vision. But with the glasses and everything else, he looks like a different person, and I imagine that's the intended effect. *If I've transformed this much on the outside, imagine what I'm like on the inside. My feelings about you have changed irrevocably.*

I didn't even consider my appearance before leaving the house. I'm just the same old Solvig. Short, unkempt hair, old jeans, faded sweatshirt, parka, frown.

James isn't wearing a coat. He's in a navy fisherman's jumper with the sleeves rolled up. He looks so huggable that I have to keep my hands in my pockets.

He stops before he reaches me. "Good morning, Solvig. Shall we walk?"

Why yes, Mr. Darcy, I think sarcastically. *Let's perambulate.*

"I thought you found neck tattoos too full-on," I say, as we begin to stride.

"It's the god Khepri."

"Not a dung beetle, then."

"He pushed the sun across the sky."

"Like a ball of dung." I thrust my hands into my pockets, listening to the sound of the waves. *This too shall pass.*

"Look, Solvig, I've got some stuff I need to talk to you about," says James. I know it's not that long since I last saw him—less than two months—but I'd almost forgotten about the way his hands jerk out when he's building up to disclosing something. I've seen him do it a thousand times before, but it seems so intoxicating when accompanied by the threat of never seeing him again.

"I was the one that asked to meet up," I say. "I need to talk to you. But you go first if you like. I'd like to hear what you have to say." Actually, I don't want to hear a word of it. I want to say my piece, and then I want James to hold me until I stop hurting.

"Let's head onto the beach," James says, pointing at some steps leading down to the sand. "Don't tread on anything that looks like a plastic bag. Portuguese man-o'-wars have been washing up lately. Their tentacles—which are venomous, by the way—can be over thirty metres long."

Even at a time like this, James can't resist explaining something to me. He must have told me about the Portuguese man-o'-war's venomous tentacles at least half a dozen times since we met. And how the creature is not even technically an *it* but rather a *they*. A colony of organisms working together.

I'll be sad if James never explains anything to me ever again. I used to see his lectures as a little conceited. Maybe he's just interested in things, and he wanted to share those interests with me. I wish I'd shared more with him in return.

"I've been thinking about what you told me," James says as we walk towards the sea. "About what happened in Liverpool. On your dive. About you cheating on me."

It stings to hear James get the facts wrong. He's getting them wrong because I haven't been honest with him.

"I'm angry with you, Solvig," he continues. "You should have talked to me. Relationships need communication. And given your job, and you having to go away so often . . . I need to know where your mind is. I don't want to hear about where your body's been once it's already too late."

"You're right," I say, stepping over a crushed Coke can.

James stops gesticulating. His arms fall limp by his side. "This thing that occurred, between you and the woman. It's indicative of a much bigger problem between us."

I wait for James to say more, but he doesn't. I want to beg him to explain something to me, whether it's how the Portuguese man-o'-war's digestive system works, or how to save our relationship, but there's only silence.

That time we were in the Lake District, when our relationship was a fragile bud, James shared something. "I've only ever been broken up with," he disclosed, as we watched our camp-fire's dying embers. "I've never been the one to end a relation-ship." At the time, I found his words comforting. If I ended up breaking up with him, I figured, I'd be one of a long line of women who had done the same. Now, with the benefit of hindsight, I know what James's confession really was. It was a warning.

When we reach the sea, we stop and look at the waves. I dip my toe in the water. James presses his shoe into the wet sand and draws a line in it.

We turn and start walking along the beach.

"James," I say, launching into the piece I've been practising all the way here. "When I'm on land, I want to be in the sea. When I'm happy, I'm waiting to be sad. When I'm here, I'm looking over there." I point towards the far end of the beach, towards Newlyn, but really, I'm thinking about Mars. "It's a way of trying not to feel trapped."

"You felt trapped with me? Because I never—"

"It's a trap of my own making. I've always had one foot in and one out. But I don't want that any more. When I'm here, I want to be here. And when I'm gone . . ."

"Gone?"

"I mean, in the future. If my work takes me, you know, far away."

"Further than the North Sea?" James sounds wary, and weary.

"I'll give up diving," I say, as though ripping off a plaster. "Being shut away for a month at a time probably isn't good for me. I used to think I could stay locked in that chamber forever.

Recently, I've realised how much I need the stuff on the outside too."

"Right," says James. I know that look. I saw him doing it after a regular customer started spreading rumours about him using unclean needles, then came into the studio one day, tail between his legs, asking for a new tattoo. It was a look that said *too late for that now.*

I stop walking. I taste the salt and smell the seaweed and feel the breeze. "James," I say. "I'm pregnant."

James looks at me blankly. Then his eyes flash with a series of emotions, like I'm watching them tick along on a zoetrope. Confusion. Disbelief. Horror.

"It's from the last time we . . . I haven't known for long."

James turns away from me, towards the town. I think he's looking in the direction of his parents' house. When he turns back, his voice is almost inaudible. "I've been trying to break up with you."

I look down at my hands, tinged blue in the cold, and I take off my eternity ring. The flesh is indented where the ring used to be. It's worn me away.

I hold it tight in my fist; then I offer it to James. Automatically, he takes it, and I catch sight of the ouroboros tattoo on his forearm.

"The relationship isn't healthy for either of us," he says.

"Not at the moment."

"How do you feel about the pregnancy?"

"Scared."

We sit down on the sand, even though it's damp and it's going to stick to our clothes. Feels good to be grounded. I wonder if James is going to put his arm around me, but he doesn't. We stare out at the horizon in silence.

At last, I say: "I've got an interview next week, in America. I entered that competition you told me about. To be one of the first people to go and live on Mars."

James stares at me. And then he begins to laugh.

I laugh too.

Soon, we are laughing uncontrollably, shrieking and roaring and grabbing fistfuls of sand, then watching the grains fall between our splayed fingers.

•

In the car, I scream behind a closed mouth.

"I'll support you whatever you decide," James said after a stiff hug on the promenade. "Whatever you decide": it's obvious he was referring to an abortion. "We'll make it work whatever happens," he said after that. "Whatever happens": he meant it's over.

"Whatever," I say now, under my breath, before I start the car.

I'm not proud of myself for the way I drive back to Falmouth. I get beeped at three times, and I have to do an emergency stop at a roundabout.

When I switch off the engine outside the doctor's surgery, I notice how loudly I'm breathing.

"Fuck. Shit. Fucking arse shit."

I get out of the car and head for reception. "Appointment, please," I say, wiping sand off the back of my coat.

The man behind the desk takes my name and date of birth and asks whom I'd like to see. "Computers are down," he explains. "Got to do it the old-fashioned way." He opens a diary and licks the tip of his finger every time he turns the page. He finds an appointment for two weeks' time.

"I was hoping for something sooner," I say.

"Ah." He looks over his glasses. "It's an emergency appointment?"

I think about heart attacks and appendicitis and gangrene. "No. It's not an emergency." I take the appointment and leave.

I sit in the car, still breathing heavily, and I pick up my phone.

"Are you at home?" I ask when Anouk answers.

"I'm just coming out of Tesco," she says. "Solvig, what's up? I haven't heard from you in ages. You won't answer my texts. James has gone AWOL too. Did he find out about Mars?"

"James and I split up," I say. "I nearly slept with this woman. Then I had a miscarriage. Now I'm pregnant again." I look at my reflection in the rear-view mirror. "I hate myself, Anouk. I hate myself for bringing a child into this terrible mess."

It annoys me that Anouk doesn't agree with me. "You poor thing," she says. "Why didn't you tell me? Do you want to come round for a cuppa? I've just bought a multipack of Kit Kats."

"I need some alone time," I tell her. "I'll call you tomorrow."

I sit in the car park for a few minutes, waiting for my heart rate to decrease, and then I drive home. I'm sensible and generous, letting cars out in front of me wherever I can. Each time someone raises a hand to thank me, I feel like a slightly better person. *If two more people thank me on the drive home, I'll keep it.*

I let three more cars out in front of me, but only the first driver raises his hand.

When I get home, I climb the stairs and go straight to bed. I'm surprised to find Cola lying on James's side. His eyes are open, unblinking.

I lie down and spoon him.

"Hello, baby. You're all right now. It's over." I stroke his velvety ears, his shaggy muzzle, his rigid body.

34

I must have fallen asleep with the bathroom light on. It's giving my skin a bleached, otherworldly glow. My dead dog is in bed with me. His lank fur is pressed against my shoulder. He smells of the juice at the bottom of a bin.

When I lie on my back, my stomach becomes a hammock slung between my hip bones. Tonight, though, there's something different about it. Just below my navel, and slightly to the left, there's a bulge. Looks like I've swallowed a lump of moon rock.

I need to get up.

I put on something warm; then I go downstairs and down two glasses of water. I slip my feet into my laced-up trainers and head into the garden.

In spite of James's attempts to get me into gardening, it's been ages since I've been in the shed. It's so tidy in here. I grab the spade and begin to dig smack bang in the middle of a flower bed. "Cyclamen are a great food source for caterpillars," James told me when he planted them last year.

I've never buried anything before. I'm not sure how deep you're supposed to go. I can make out only basic shapes using the light from the kitchen window—but no doubt I'm digging up worms and grubs. I wonder what they think is happening, suddenly being thrust out into the cold air.

The hole becomes so deep that in order to continue digging, I need to climb in. I dig until the ground is level with my knees; then I sit in my man-made crater as though it's a bathtub. I rest my head on a pillow of dirt and look up at the sky. I can see the Big Dipper and, using that, the North Star. I'm pretty sure that one of the other bright objects in the sky is Betelgeuse. You can tell by the reddish tint.

It's time to bury my dog.

I leave a trail of soil all the way up the stairs and into my bedroom. When I put my arms around Cola, I hear him exhale.

"You alive, boy?"

He looks like a taxidermy animal, like an imitation of a dog I once had. He's definitely not alive; his carcass must have released air when moved. I carry him downstairs carefully, nervous that he'll leak something dead onto me.

As I lower him into the hole, I wonder if I should say a few words. We never had a funeral for my mum. We gave her a direct cremation, without a service. When I was old enough to discover that's what Dad had chosen for her, I assumed he was being a cheapskate. When I think about it now, I don't want a funeral either. I want to explode in a blaze of glory, then disappear into the ether.

I run back into the house and grab something I've been keeping stuffed behind the recipe books in the kitchen: the onesie. I let it fall onto my dog's frozen haunches, and then I bury the whole lot, until I am looking at nothing but earth.

•

The ocean is hidden by clouds, but that doesn't change anything. Fact is, there are people walking on the seafloor at this very moment. There are sharks and manatees and humpback whales and seahorses swimming in every direction.

I have a tray of food in front of me. Tarragon chicken with dauphinoise potatoes; couscous salad; a bread roll; cream crackers; a rectangle of mild cheddar; chocolate mousse. Every element makes me feel sick. The chicken is the worst, though. It makes me think of battery hens, crammed into tiny cages, their bald skin rubbed free of feathers.

"Seems a little early for lunch." The passenger next to me nods at my uneaten food. In front of her is a selection of vegetarian curries. Smashed lentils, bruised veg, sauces bleeding into one another.

I smile. "Yes, exactly."

"They've got a lot to get through, I expect." The woman nibbles a pakora. "Still, it'll be a while before we get to DC. And I'm not sure if we get dinner."

"I'm pregnant," I blurt. "The baby isn't an embryo any more. It's a foetus."

The woman raises her eyebrows, then points at my chicken. "Better keep up your strength in that case."

"Can I ask you something? It's kind of personal."

The woman turns towards me. She has laughter lines and prematurely grey hair. It's possible she's dyed it that colour on purpose. "Go ahead."

"What made you decide to go vegetarian?"

She laughs. "I thought you were going to ask my age. Or if I've got kids." She pours a tiny bottle of Gordon's gin into a plastic cup full of ice. "Global warming, mainly."

"Do you ever miss meat?"

"Only at Thanksgiving." She adds a can of tonic to the cup and takes a sip. "But then I miss the whole shebang. My mom's buttered rum. My dad's corny jokes. Watching the parade. Sitting by the fire. Remembering to be thankful . . . Anyway, the whole stealing-land-off-Native-Americans, mass-genocide thing leaves a sour taste in my mouth. I'm better off saving my Tofurky for Christmas."

"I work in the oil industry," I say. "Maybe I should go vegetarian."

"Well." The woman shrugs. "You've got to figure out what matters to you. And how you want to make a difference."

I look out of the window and notice a gap in the clouds. I can see the ocean now, flat as concrete. I close my eyes.

I've no idea how long they stay shut.

When I open them, my tray has gone. The woman next to me has gone. Outside, there's nothing but dust. Red, swirling, full of possibility.

"Let me tell you a story, little one," I say, placing my hand over my belly. "It's about the very first woman to set foot on Mars."

ACKNOWLEDGMENTS

Thank you to Masie Cochran for your wise editorial advice, and for helping me to enjoy hitting the delete button. Thank you to Anne Horowitz for your amazingly thorough copyediting, and everyone at Tin House for believing in me. Thank you to Claire Friedman at Inkwell Management for representing me in the US, and to my UK agent Juliet Pickering at Blake Friedmann for your amazing input as always, as well as Hattie Grunewald and James Sykes—it's been wonderful to work with such a great team. Thank you to Kirstin Innes and Julia Moreno for putting better words into my characters' mouths. Thank you to Athina and Ron Adams-Florou for giving me my Thursdays back, and to Sue and Kirsten Mackintosh for babysitting and believing in me. Thank you to Apollo MacAdams for (sometimes) taking naps to let me finish this. Also, Apollo: thank you for blowing my life apart. I mean it. Thank you to Socrates Adams for your unwavering love and support. I'm glad we are in this place together.

READER'S GUIDE

1. In your own life, would you ever be interested in going to Mars?

2. How would you describe the relationship between Solvig and James? When she says, "he wouldn't be in love with me if I were the sort of person who didn't go away regularly. And I wouldn't love him if I stayed," what do you think she means?

3. How does the novel explore the interplay between motherhood and ambition?

4. Would you classify this book as science fiction or futuristic? How much does the future, as presented by the book, already feel part of our present moment?

5. How do the stories Solvig's been told about her mother, and Solvig's current relationship with her father, affect the choices that she makes throughout the novel?

6. What role does fear play in this book? Which character do you think is the most afraid?

7. In a hypothetical group exercise, Solvig announces that she'd want to live, while others say they'd sacrifice themselves if it meant lightening the load of their transit vehicle on Mars. Do you agree with the way that Solvig, or the others, responded? Is there such a thing as a "correct" response in this situation?

8. What do you think Solvig decides to do at the end of the novel?

9. Was Solvig right to keep her interest in Mars from James for so long? Why or why not?

10. In real life, author Anneliese Mackintosh's father worked for the European Space Agency (ESA). In what ways do you think his experience might have informed this narrative?

PHOTO: SOCRATES ADAMS

ANNELIESE MACKINTOSH's short stories have won the UK's Green Carnation Prize, been shortlisted for the Edge Hill Prize, and longlisted for the Frank O'Connor International Short Story Award. She lives in Bristol, England, with her husband, son, and two cats.